ONCE A GRASS WIDOW:
Watchekee's Destiny

George Godfrey

Nishnabek Publications
2013

Nishnabek Publications
24108 Burr Oaks Lane, Athens, Illinois, USA

Copyright © 2013 by George L. Godfrey

Cover design by Ticara

All rights reserved. No part of this publication may be reproduced, stored in a retrieval system, or transmitted, in any form or by any means, electronic, mechanical, photocopying, recording, or otherwise, without the prior written permission from the author, except for the inclusion of brief quotations in a review.

ISBN 978-1-48253-854-0

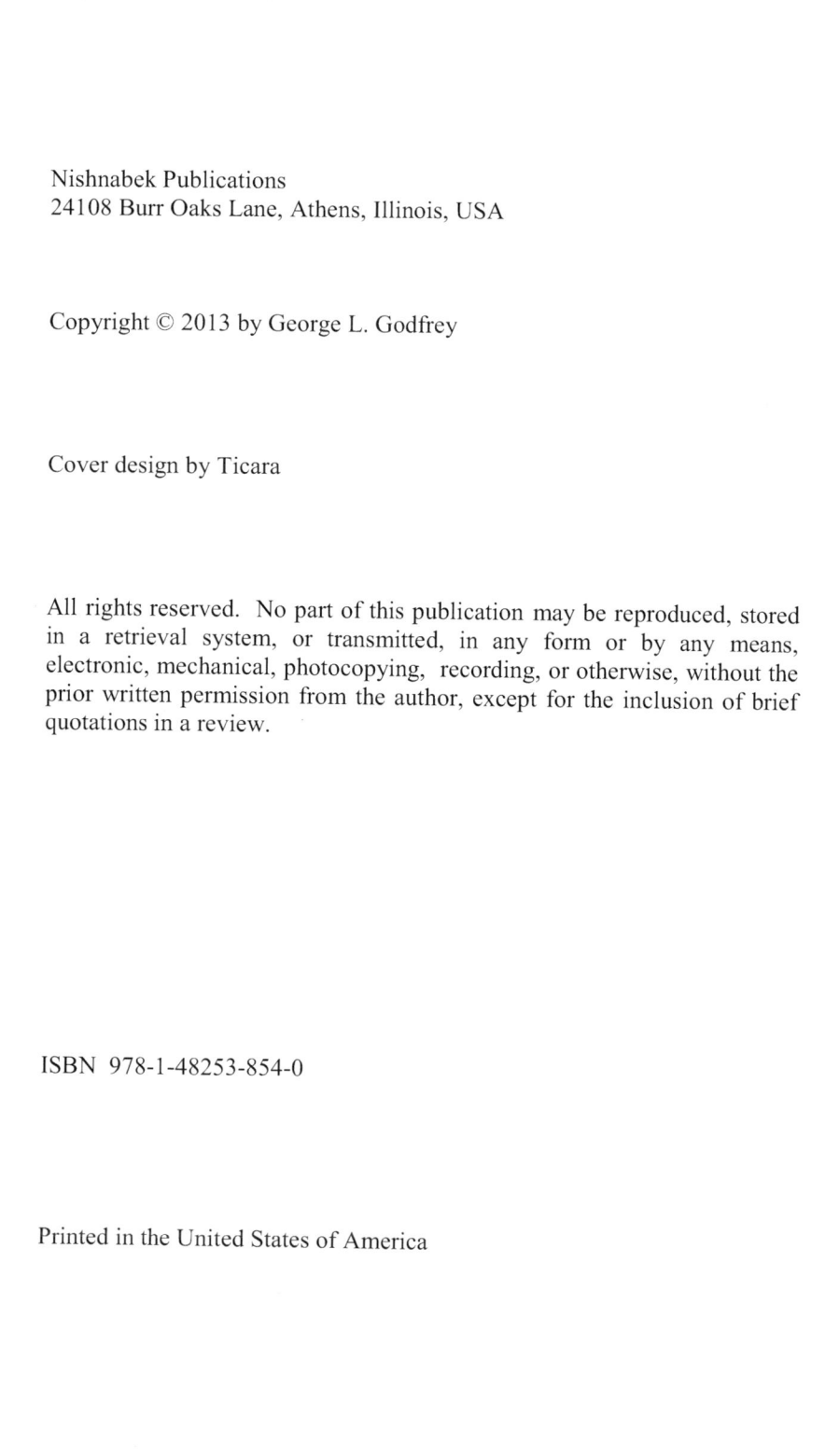

Printed in the United States of America

To my children

Three to nine — depending on how you count

Tom, Darren, Cheree
Bret, Jill, Pegè
Andrea, Erika, Regina

Contents

Acknowledgments vi
Foreword vii
Prologue viii
Chapters
  1 - Surviving 1
  2 - Return to Bourbonnais Grove 7
  3 - Arranged Marriage 13
  4 - Powder Medicine 17
  5 - Zozzette, Josette — Etta 23
  6 - No More Hurt 27
  7 - Kickapoo Village 31
  8 - Uncle Sid 35
  9 - Goin' to Join My Wife 38
  10 - Emerging From the Wigwam 42
  11 - Them Half-Breeds? 46
  12 - Kankakee River Valley 51
  13 - Purple Mist 55
  14 - Quito's Reply 60
  15 - Her Fate 65
  16 - Possible Attack 69
  17 - Cross Creek Bridge 74
  18 - White Man's Politics 78
  19 - The Shootings 84
  20 - Three Oaks 91
  21 - The Tannery 99
  22 - Bag of Gold 104
  23 - Homecoming 107
  24 - Horde of Grasshoppers 113
  25 - Lieutenant Murphy's Message 116
  26 - The Post Surgeon 120
  27 - Walked All the Way 125
  28 - Mr. Bergeron! Mr. Bergeron! 132
  29 - K-K-K-Kate! 138
  30 - Talk With Moke-je-win 142
  31 - Journey's Over 146
  32 - Left Alone 151
  33 - Tell Me About It 155
  34 - The Exploration 159
  35 - Seven Families 168
  36 - The Tornado 173
  37 - Arbuckle Wagon Road 178
  38 - Lifeless Body 182

Acknowledgments

Improvements of this writing as it entered its final phases were made by Noel Greenwalt through his meticulous editing and candid advice. The same can be said for my wife, Pat, and who also unselfishly gave me latitude for the MANY nights that I stayed up late either writing or revising the text. Larry Upton, Ralph Bazhaw and Lana Ball provided information useful in understanding the history of the Bergeron family; and Gerald Born that of the Vail family. Sharon Hoogstraten not only took the photograph of me that appears on the back cover, see "About the Author," but also gave me permission to use it. Several of the Potawatomi names used in this fictional history were taken from the 1863 Potawatomi Tribal Roll. Usage of the names does not imply that all were involved in the factual parts of the following story.

Foreword

This fictional historical writing is based on the life of Watchekee (pronounced *Watch-e-key*), wife of Francis Xavier Bergeron and the ancestral mother of many persons within the Citizen Potawatomi Nation. Starting with known factual information, I have blended family oral history. To these have been added a liberal sprinkling of imaginative situations and conversational dialogue in an effort to help readers, whether they be Watchekee's descendents or other interested persons, better follow Watchekee's life. Hopefully, the text will provide a glimpse of how Watchekee may have dealt with the society or societies in which she found herself and the influence that her family — even indirectly one Civil War campaign — may have had on where the Citizen Potawatomi established their reservation in the Indian Territory.

Prologue

Watchekee found herself in the midst of survival, not only for herself, but also for her children. The totality of her experiences unknowingly contributed to the history of the Citizen Potawatomi Nation. The emotional, economic and cultural struggles that she faced, as well as her life-time experiences, cannot be measured. Surely, they were heavy or numerous, regardless of how one may choose to measure them. Strands of her life crossed many boundaries: traditional Potawatomi life in Illinois, a 'pawn' in trader-tribal economic relations, single motherhood, economics of destituteness and wealth, politics of freedom versus slavery, religion and reservation life. Her death may have come at the expense of protecting her French Canadian husband, Francis Xavier Bergeron. If protecting the one she loved was involved, the history behind the name, Watchekee, can be amplified farther than its original bestowment.

1 – Surviving

Mixed emotions swarmed through thirty year-old Watchekee as she stood by her horse. She was preparing to depart from the Loess Hills in western Iowa Territory and undertake a long ride back to Bourbonnais Grove in northeastern Illinois. Leaving meant the loss of social and family support from other Potawatomi. However, in her mind, such support all but had vanished because the culture in which she had been raised in Illinois was now in social and economic disarray.

Uprooting the Potawatomi from their homelands in the Great Lakes States had turned many of them into goalless and shiftless persons. Fights over alcohol and murders were not uncommon. There was the additional wariness because the Yankton Sioux occasionally made violent raids into the new Potawatomi lands. Watchekee decided that it would be best for her and her children to escape the madness and return to Bourbonnais Grove. More importantly in her mind, she emotionally was driven to find and see Noel in Illinois. After all, he was the father of her children, but she was not the mother of all of them.

Close friends of Watchekee, Archange Peltier and Joseph Babeu, expressed similar sentiments to her in late spring 1840. They made their feelings known when the three of them were visiting at the St. Joseph Mission on the Council Bluffs Reservation.

Watchekee's friendship with Archange started when Archange helped Watchekee deliver her baby girl in Princeton, Illinois. Because of the help that Watchekee got from Archange, she named her baby after her. This happened during their removal in 1837 along with hundreds of other Potawatomi from northeastern Illinois. Later, Archange and Joseph became godparents of Watchekee, her children or extended family members. In so doing, they became part of Watchekee's family, not just friends.

As Archange and Joseph reined in their horses beside Watchekee, Joseph saw the other horses she had tied to tree branches beside her wigwam and straight forwardly asked, "Watchekee, only three more?"

Just then four children, Will (nine), Elihu (eight), Olivie (five) and young Archange (three), came out of Watchekee's wigwam, rubbing their eyes, adjusting them to the bright sunlight.

"Well," replied Watchekee, "one, as you can see, is loaded with supplies. We'll need them for our trip. The other two are for my children. They're too young to walk all the way back to Illinois."

Joseph already knew that Watchekee's children were going, but asked, "Shouldn't there be four horses so that each child will have one?"

Watchekee had anticipated Joseph's question and answered, "The boys are old enough to ride by themselves. The girls aren't, so each boy will have one of his sisters ride with him. Besides, my father, Shabonee, could only give me three horses. He'll be going back to Illinois himself in just a few weeks and will need the rest of his horses for himself and the people who are goin' with him."

****

The wigwam from which the four children emerged had sheltered them since they and their mother were escorted back to Council Bluffs from the Kickapoo village north of Fort Leavenworth the previous December. The weather was bitterly cold and snow was falling then.

Watchekee and her four children went to live with the Kickapoo in Kansas shortly after the baptisms of Olivie and Archange in 1837. However, she soon was labeled as an indigent and a "grass widow." It was deemed that she belonged on the Council Bluffs Reservation and, thus, was returned to it by Major Hitchcock. Although welcomed back by her father and enjoying the physical warmth of his wigwam, Watchekee still suffered from dejection and tremendous inner turmoil.

Watchekee's troubled feelings started when Noel threw her out in early 1837. *"At least,"* she thought as her children in their young, oblivious minds drifted to sleep under layers of blankets, *"they're safe and warm."* Late one winter night, she determinably thought, *"We'll survive!"*

The Neshbotna River flows west and empties into the Missouri River in southwestern Iowa. Watchekee was thankful that her village, located near the Neshbotna River, was several miles from the Missouri. However, the one disadvantage of her village's location is that it was quite distant from the headquarters of the Council Bluffs Agency, which was on the Nebraska side of the Missouri. Consequently, travelling to it and returning home on the same day was difficult and tiring.

While returning from the agency where she had gone to get her annual annuity payment, Watchekee ventured to Steamboat Landing on the east bank of the Missouri to watch the arrival of a paddle-wheeler. She was aghast at what unfolded when the river boat docked. Somehow, some of the 2,000 Potawatomi who had congregated there knew that the boat's cannons were loaded with whiskey and rum. A fight broke out over the illegal cargo even before the lines of the river boat could be thrown to waiting hands on the loading dock. During the melee, noses of some of the combatants were slashed or cut off. It was a technique commonly used by Potawatomi fighters to dispatch non-tribal opponents, not other Potawatomi.

Upset by what she saw, Watchekee and her children

took refuge in Billy Caldwell's village, which was a short distance east of the Missouri, rather than return directly to her own village on the Neshbotna. Thoughts of the fighting Watchekee witnessed at Steamboat Landing kept reoccurring to her throughout the night. The din of singing katydids and the hot humid summer night added to Watchekee's inability to sleep soundly. Visions of peacefulness along the Kankakee River in Illinois also flashed through Watchekee's mind. Half awake, she thought to herself, *"Will I ever again live the tranquility and happiness that I had with Noel in Bourbonnais Grove?"*

****

    Will and Elihu gleefully went to their mounts when instructed to do so by their mother. Because the boys were still young and being unable to leap onto their horses' backs from a standing jump, they led their horses to a tree stump and climbed on. Still it was comical to see the boys throw their torsos onto the backs of their horses and for each to finally get into a comfortable riding position. There was a brief moment of indecision as to which sister was to ride with which brother.
    "Let me help," said Joseph as he dismounted and took Olivie by the hand and boosted her up to ride behind Will. "There you go!" Next he put Archange behind Elihu. "It's going to be a long trip, and you can change!" Watchekee and her friend, the older Archange, sat on their horses smiling at the way Joseph organized the younger members of the entourage. With everything set, the group started up the valley of the Neshbotna and back to Illinois.
    Watchekee's estranged marital relations with Noel LeVasseur were foremost in her mind as she crossed over the last of the Loess Hills and entered the rolling prairies of southern Iowa Territory. Their relationship started after she returned from Missouri where she had gone with the Kickapoo

from Danville, Illinois, in the late 1820's. It was strange because before she left with the Kickapoo, she was married to Gurdon Hubbard, Noel's boss in the fur trading business.

Watchekee actually was Noel's second wife because his first wife, Mesawkequa, still was with him when Watchekee became a member of the household. Watchekee and Mesawkequa were sisters and the polygamous triad was a norm by tribal standards. One of Watchekee's children by Noel, Archange, was born in the relative comforts of their log cabin at Bourbonnais Grove. Two more children were in the same household, Will and Marianne. Their mother actually was Mesawkequa. William Chobart, a fur trader who worked with Noel, was Will's father, but Noel was the father of Marianne After Mesawkequa left the area with the Bourbonnais family in 1835, Auntie Watchekee took care of Marianne Will and, by tribal standards, became their mother.

Suddenly in early 1837, Noel told Watchekee to leave. Little did he know that she was pregnant with little Archange at the time. Watchekee didn't even know. Because of these circumstances and her destituteness when she first found herself in Council Bluffs and later at Fort Leavenworth, Watchekee was considered to be an indigent and a "grass widow" by the U.S. Army, which then oversaw all Indian affairs.

For a short time, Mesawkequa also lived near Ft. Leavenworth but moved to Council Bluffs where she and Watchekee reunited. They had countless visits, often about Noel.

"Is Noel still in Bourbonnais Grove?" asked Mesawkequa. "You know I left him, but don't really know why."

"Yes, I remember," replied Watchekee. "As far as I know he is still there. He threw me and the children out two years after you left — never gave me a reason — just threw us out. It was cold, really cold when he told me to leave. About the only thing I could do was go to my father's village up north of Bourbonnais Grove. I took most of the children with me, including Will of course, but Noel made Marianne stay."

It was during her conversations with Mesawkequa that Watchekee began wondering if Noel would take her back. The burning thought partially fueled her plans to return to Bourbonnais Grove.

2 – Return to Bourbonnais Grove

Watchekee, her children, and friends reached Big Foot's village, several miles up the Neshbotna River, the first night during their return to Illinois. Big Foot and his people had removed themselves from southern Wisconsin. The reason they went by themselves was because Big Foot didn't want to be under the direction of Lewis Sands who was to have been their removal conductor. Big Foot detested Sands ever since meeting him during the negotiations of the Chicago Treaty of 1833, which resulted in the loss of Potawatomi land holdings in northern Illinois and southeastern Wisconsin. Big Foot further shunned federal authorities by spending the first year in central Iowa after leaving Wisconsin rather than going to the reservation at Council Bluffs. He eventually moved his band of Potawatomi to the Council Bluffs Reservation, but he and his band stayed in the eastern side of it.

Big Foot was surprised when Watchekee and her small group rode into his village. Ignoring her, he asked Joseph, "Did you see any Sioux? They've been coming down from the north and attacking some of our people."

"No," replied Joseph. "We had no problems. We're going back to Illinois and left Shabonee's village this morning,"

Watchekee and Archange concurred with Joseph. Watchekee quickly said, "We had a safe ride." Archange simply nodded her head.

Big Foot frowned when he heard the name Shabonee, but soon began acting like a gracious host to his guests.

Will and Elihu helped their sisters down to ground. They then slid off led their horses, gathered up the reins of the horses that the adults had ridden and led all the animals to the Neshbotna River so they could drink. After the mounts drank for several minutes, while stomping their hooves and swishing their tails to get rid of pesky deer flies, Will and Elihu took the horses to an expansive prairie covered with big blue stem grass, prairie rocket and goldenrod that was showing blossom buds. After hobbling the steeds, Will and Elihu looked around for Olivie and little Archange. Their sisters already had joined some of the village children in a game of who could catch the most grasshoppers. Seeing the activity underway, Will and Elihu ran to join in.

Mainly to alleviate his fear of possible marauding Sioux and the harm that they might cause to such a small group of Potawatomi protected by just one man, Big Foot offered the services of twenty men when he fed his guests. Looking at Joseph as the visitor's leader, Big Foot while standing in front of his wigwam said, "My men will escort you and your group to the Yellow Banks along the Mississippi River. That's where I crossed the big river three years ago."

Joseph simply said, "Thanks."

The men, chosen from the ranks of the red moiety (secondborns) for the task, felt honored and eagerly rode out at dawn the next morning with the small group who had come from Shabonee's village. Zah-kto was designated as the escort's leader by Big Foot.

At one point during the ride to the Mississippi River, Zah-kto stopped. Slowly he approached the Skunk River. Joseph quickly rode up to him and asked, "What's the problem? Is there danger?" "No," replied Zah-kto, who had a rather nostalgic look on his face. "We spent the first year here after leaving Wisconsin." After a brief pause, Zah-kto signaled for the others to move on by merely nodding his head forward.

The remainder of the ride to the Mississippi River took several days. Only once were the travelers delayed. The delay was not due to inclement weather but rather by a herd of moving buffalo. Everybody had to wait until the herd passed. When the Mississippi River came into view, it looked like a formidable obstacle blocking Watchekee's quest to return to Illinois.

Zah-kto, realizing the group's apprehension, turned to Joseph and said in a reassuring voice, "You can cross here this time of the year." He and the rest of the escort men then turned and headed back to Big Foot's village in the direction of the setting sun.

Joseph then nudged his horse into the Mississippi and said, "Illinois is on the other side! Watchekee, you take little Archange! Archange, Olivie! Boys, get a good grip on your horses' manes and don't let go — even if you fall off! I will keep my horse as close to yours as possible! Everybody, once we get into the river let the horses do the work! They'll know how to swim if we get into deep water! Don't worry about the pack horse. She will follow the other horses."

Fording the Mississippi River went more smoothly than expected, but everyone was exhausted from excitement and nervousness. Seeing the condition of the other travelers, Joseph said, "Let's find a grassy clearing above the river bank and stay there for the night. All of our camping supplies are wet so we'll have to sleep without any blankets or tents and put up with the mosquitoes. I'll find something for us to eat."

The evening meal looked like it was going to be the mussels that Watchekee and Archange collected along a sandbar in a sluggish backwater pool of the river. Much to Watchekee's delight, Will and Elihu had snared three ground squirrels and skinned them before she returned from the river. Still, the paucity of just three ground squirrels and a handful of clams did not appear very ample for the hungry travelers.

Just as the sun began setting, Joseph came riding into camp. His shirt was lumpy and dangled from his horse's withers. Chickens, which had their legs bound, flopped unceremoniously behind his saddle.

Watchekee and Archange were beginning to roast their meager meal over an open fire when Joseph arrived. Expecting Joseph to return with a deer, Watchekee stood up and stared in disbelief and open-mouthed at the scene that she and the others were seeing.

"*What* did you get?" asked Watchekee as she looked wide-eyed at Joseph's cargo.

Grinning, Joseph said, "Seven eggs and three chickens!"

Archange, joining in, asked, "Where?"

Carefully handing the shirt full of eggs to Archange and the bewildered-looking chickens to Watchekee, Joseph began explaining, "There's a settler's cabin down that way." He pursed his lips and pointed downstream. "No one was around. Either the owner won't mind sharing or he'll think that a skunk or fox got his missing chickens!"

The yelps and cries of coyotes filled the ears of Watchekee. She eventually drifted off to sleep, no blanket, stomach full from the land's bounty and the unknowing graciousness of a white settler, and mind full of images regarding Noel. "*What'll he think when he sees me?*"

The warmth and light of the rising sun's rays awakened Watchekee the next morning, yet she felt the chill brought on by heavy dew. As she stirred, she saw Joseph and Archange snuggling by a fire they had started a few minutes earlier. The children were still asleep as if in one ball of human flesh. Sleeping in this fashion, they seemingly were immune to the morning's coolness and dampness.

Watchekee got up from where she had slept and sought out the privacy of a clump of bushes, a short distance from the camp. Walking back to the warmth of the fire, she sat down next to Archange, and while looking straight ahead she asked, "Joseph, how long will it take to get to Bourbonnais Grove?"

"I figure that Bourbonnais Grove is about seven days

away. Several trails cross this part of Illinois so we should be able to travel faster than we did in Iowa. In about two days, we should get to a little village called Galesburg," remarked Joseph.

"I think I remember the place," commented Watchekee. "We went through it when we were removed in 1837."

"How's that?" asked Joseph.

****

Eventually, as Watchekee, her children and travelling companions were crossing the Illinois River by picking their way across the rocky rapids downstream from LaSalle, Archange asked, "Watchekee, do you remember this area?"

"Yes," replied Watchekee. "Little Archange was born near here. It was near Princeton on the 1837 removal. Some of us said here that we should go straight west, but we were taken on a route that looked like a snake crawling." Dreadful memories of the trip in 1837 began to cycle through Watchekee's mind, *"I don't know how I got the children to Council Bluffs alive — lots of rain and mud just after we crossed the Mississippi River — flooding in Missouri — collapsed bridge — wading deep water to cross a flooded area — lost little girl — her poor mother was told that she couldn't stop and look for her."*

The land started to become more and more familiar to Watchekee as the trail, which had now become a well-worn wagon road, passed through Wilmington along the Kankakee River. *"By tomorrow, I'll be in Bourbonnais Grove — home!"* thought Watchekee.

Bourbonnais Grove slowly came into view. Watchekee seemed confused when she arrived and stopped her horse where her cabin had been in early 1837. She sat motionless, staring at a two-story brick house.

Joseph and Archange also reined in their horses. Finally, Joseph said to Watchekee, "I hope that everything goes all right. Archange and me are going on to Joliet so we'll say good-bye now."

After tears and hugs on the dusty wagon road leading past the brick house, Joseph and Archange slowly disappeared as they rode northward. Watchekee was left on the wagon road with her children. She was not alone physically, but alone emotionally as thoughts of Noel began to pour into her soul.

Finally, Watchekee turned to her children and said, "Wait here." She then dismounted and walked up to the front door. Opening the door without knocking, Watchekee came face to face with a white woman clutching an infant.

3 – Arranged Marriage

Noel had a problem — a big problem. For several years, he thought that he permanently had cast aside Watchekee and did not ever expect to see her again. To his utter disbelief, she had returned, not only with the children that he knew were his but with a fourth child that she said was his. His wife of a formal marriage was not pleased with the encounter with and the new knowledge of Watchekee.

Perhaps as a means of resolving the situation, Noel headed his buggy northwest to seek the advice of William Rantz who ran a mill that served as a store and engaged in other entrepreneurships in the surrounding rural community.

White settlers in the area used to call William 'Bill' until he sold them some rancid meat. After that they started calling him by his last name, Rantz. At first, he was miffed when he found out the connection with the meat that he had sold and his family name. He later found the humor in the situation, especially when he realized the notoriety that he had received actually increased his business.

Noel felt very much at ease at Rantz's because it was near there where he brought in other French Canadian immigrants to settle in the Kankakee River Valley. In exchange for the cost that he incurred for their immigration, he required them to work for him for one year. It was good for his lucrative and expanding real estate business. The presence of another wife, especially one who was Potawatomi, could be a real impediment to his lofty financial goals.

Noel was glad when he saw Rantz standing in front of his mill. Pulling up his buggy and hitching his horses to a rail that protected Rantz's garden, Noel said in a "put-on" cheery voice laced with an accent that betrayed his French Canadian origins, "Good morning, Bill."

"Hi, Noel!" responded Rantz, somewhat surprised to see Noel so early in the day. "What brings you out here?"

Noel glanced around and quietly asked, "Rantz, can we talk in private?"

"Of course! Let's go and sit under the elm over there," offered Rantz as he gestured for Noel to lead the way. He wondered what was on Noel's mind as they sat down and asked, "What's happening?"

The softly-swaying branches of the giant elm beside Rantz's store and the sweet smell of his grain mill belied the dilemma that Noel was in. In almost a groan, Noel said, "Bill, Watchekee's back. I tried to entice her to go back to Council Bluffs with some money and with several pots and blankets from my store. After that I told her that anything between us was over. She still won't leave. To make matter worse, Watchekee set up her tent in my front yard and is staying there along with the children. Ruth wouldn't let me in the house last night or this morning, I had to sleep in the store."

Rantz started laughing.

Noel got upset and said, "It's not funny! What'm I gonna do?"

Just then a young French Canadian man rode up to Rantz's establishment on a mule. He was carefully holding a basket of eggs, and tied to the back of the saddle was a sack of shelled corn.

Noel looked at Rantz and quizzically said, "Isn't that Francois Bergeron? Does he work for you? He still owes me for arranging him to come from Montreal in 1837. Haven't been able to get'm to work for me."

Rantz answered, "Yeah, that's Francois Bergeron. He now goes by Francis. He brings in eggs for candling and corn for mashing."

"Is he married?"

"Not to my knowledge. At least he has never talked about a wife. Women are hard to find in these parts of Illinois. Didn't you bring Ruth out here all the way from Vermont?"

Hearing only the first part of what Rantz said, Noel got up and intercepted Francis just as he came back outside and started untying the sack of corn. "Francis, it's good to see you again. You sort'f disappeared after moving here," said Noel in an authoritative voice.

Francis acted surprised when Noel spoke to him and defensively answered, "Good to see you too." He continued to undo the knots and leather thongs that kept the sack of corn tied to the saddle on his mule, but avoided eye contact with Noel. He hoped that Noel would not bring up the debt that he owed him and was taken aback at what Noel next proposed. "Francis, how would like to pay your debt? I mean pay your debt as well as make some money?"

Francis turned around to look at Noel and answered, "I don't think that I heard you correctly. What'd you say?"

Without answering, Noel said, "Here, let me help you with the sack of corn," as he took the heavy sack from Francis and carried it to the masher inside Rantz's store. Francis had a look of bewilderment and skepticism on his face as he followed Noel. He knew that he owed Noel for his move from Canada, but could not figure out how he could pay his debt and make money at the same time.

Slowly, Noel said to Francis, "I know a wonderful and beautiful Potawatomi woman who would make you a good wife and needs a caring husband. She is going back to her people in Iowa. She has two very nice young daughters. If you have room in your heart to marry her, I'll forgive your debt to me *and* give you $250. You can set up your household out west. Besides, if the marriage doesn't work, just leave her and come back! No one will say anything." Noel hoped that his words would not incriminate himself, but he knew that Francis eventually would find out who was the father of Olivie and Archange. The thought of *"The boys aren't mine,"* flashed through Noel's mind.

With a curious look on his face, Francis asked, "What's her name? How did you find out about her?"

"Watchekee," Noel answered while purposefully avoiding the second question. "You don't have to give me an immediate answer. Take time to consider my offer." Noel then climbed into his buggy and drove his team back to Bourbonnais Grove. He wanted to talk to Watchekee about her future husband. He was sure that Francis would accept his offer, and he had one more enticement for Watchekee.

Finding Watchekee washing Olivie and Archange in the shallows of the Kankakee River, Noel laid out his last argument for her to leave, "I know that taking care of four children has been hard on you so I want to start supporting the boys. It wouldn't be a good idea for them to live here, but I can make arrangements for them to go to school out east — Detroit. That way, they will be able to start their own businesses someday. Also, I know a man who would be a good provider for you and the girls and will be a good husband to you."

Watchekee, having grown up in a system where marriages often were arranged, quietly acquiesced to Noel's words especially when she heard that her sons would be educated. In a subdued tone she asked, "Who?"

"Francis Bergeron," Noel answered. Externally, he seemed relieved, but internally remorseful as he sensed Watchekee's acceptance.

4 - Powder Medicine

Noel felt that a burden had been removed from his shoulders when he saw that Watchekee no longer was camped in his front yard. *"Finally,"* he thought, *"my marriage to Ruth can be salvaged, especially after I send Will and Elihu away to school!"*

Watchekee moved her camp to the spot where she knew her father, Shabonee, would be setting up a hunting village in a few weeks when he returned from Council Bluffs. The hunting village site was not far north of Rantz's mill. Unbeknownst to Watchekee, the man that she occasionally saw on a mule heading to the mill was Francis Bergeron.

Olivie and little Archange were hauling water in a bucket for Watchekee. The girls lugged the bucket, talking about turns and lengths of turns. So much water had splashed out as the girls performed their chore, that the bucket scarcely was half full by the time Watchekee got it. Watchekee was laughing at the girls when she looked up at a buggy that had pulled into the camp. Her friends, Archange and Joseph, were in it.

"I see you're riding in comfort," said Watchekee grinning and standing to greet her friends. "Did you lose your riding horses or get tired riding?"

Joseph tied the reins of the buggy horse to a tree and helped Archange get out of the buggy. After hugging Watchekee, Joseph and Archange locked arms and stepped back a few feet. Looking at Archange and then at Watchekee, Joseph said, "We got married, 'white man' style in St. Patrick's Church in Joliet by Father DuPontavice. Look! We even got a piece of paper to prove it!" They were unconcerned that Watchekee could not read! "Father DuPontavice said it's a marriage license."

Watchekee, Archange and Joseph then sat down and talked about what had happened to them since returning to Bourbonnais Grove. Their visit was filled with occasional laughter until Watchekee told Archange and Joseph about Noel.

"It's good that he offered to take care of Will and Elihu," said Watchekee. "He said he would get me a good husband."

Hearing the last comment, Archange raised her eyebrows and inquired, "What? Who?"

"Francis Bergeron, but I haven't met him yet. Don't even know what he looks like."

Archange, expressing concern for Watchekee, said "Get married white man style. He can't throw you out like LeVasseur did!"

Just as she spoke, several riders began approaching the camp. Watchekee stood up to get a better look. A big smile suddenly flashed across her face when she saw that it was her father and his party arriving from Council Bluffs for fall hunting. When Olivie and little Archange saw who arrived, they jumped up and ran to greet their grandfather.

Rantz's mill had its own visitors that day. Besides the common presence of Francis Bergeron, a circuit-riding priest from St. Patrick's Church in Joliet had arrived, Father Hippolyte DuPontavice. It was his practice to make rounds throughout his parish and perform priestly duties as called upon. He had learned and with permission from the Will County Clerk of Court to carry blank legal documents with him. They were filled out as needed and later deposited in the Clerk's office. In similar fashion, he entered Sacramental records in the books at St. Patrick's Church. His approach was somewhat unorthodox, but it fit the needs of his parish that extended many miles outside Joliet.

While he was candling eggs, Francis asked Father DuPontavice, "When will you be back?"

Father DuPontavice swirled the coffee in his pewter mug, pulled out a notebook from his robe and scrutinized it. Finally he said, "I will be back on September 14, two weeks from now."

"Good!" commented Francis as he held up another egg so that its contents could be examined, aided by the candle light behind it.

"How's that?" asked Father DuPontavice.

Francis who was sitting with his back to Father DuPontavice, turned and matter-of-factly asked "Father, can you perform a wedding then?"

"Who?" asked Father DuPontavice.

Francis sounding a bit embarrassed said, "Me."

Father DuPontavice glanced at Rantz, and jokingly said, "Me? How can you get married if there is only Me? Who is the lady?"

"Watchekee."

"She must be Potawatomi. How long have you known her?"

Taken aback, Francis said "I know of her, but haven't met her yet."

Father DuPontavice was stupefied. Looking in the direction of Rantz after staring into his now empty coffee mug, he shrugged his shoulders and said, "Fine. I'll see you on the 14th. Oh! Here, I assume."

"Yes!" answered Francis who, by this time had stepped over to mash the corn that he had brought with him and did not see Father DuPontavice's facial reaction to the answer of 'Who?'"

Just as Father DuPontavice was leaving, a petite, pretty Potawatomi woman came into Rantz's store and stood by the short counter that separated patrons from the store's merchandise.

"May I help you?" asked Rantz who had moved to his place behind the counter. He assumed this position whenever he saw a potential customer.

Much to his surprise, the small Potawatomi lady who stood before him spoke English albeit broken and with a Potawatomi cadence, "Yes. I need powder medicine."

"Powder medicine?" responded Rantz not quite understanding what the lady wanted.

Francis had finished mashing his corn in the back room. Overhearing the conversational exchange, he walked toward the counter and said, "I think the lady wants to buy some baking powder." As he pointed to a can of baking powder on the second shelf, the lady looked up at the stranger who understood what she wanted to buy and smiled appreciatively.

****

Noel sent word to Watchekee that she was to be at Rantz's place on September 14th at 11:30 a.m. or shortly before noon for her wedding. In turn, Watchekee sent a message to Joseph and Archange letting them know when and where she was going to get married. Watchekee still had not been introduced to Francis Bergeron and rightfully was nervous about the whole situation regarding a 'white man wedding.' In the past, she had been involved with men in the traditional Potawatomi way. First, it was Gurdon Hubbard. Next, it was Noel LeVasseur. Both of them were fur traders at the time of her involvement with them. Soon it was to be to Francis Bergeron, a stranger.

Francis arrived at Rantz's store on the morning of the 14th. Coming to the store, he rode his faithful mule behind his witness, Robert Duncan, who drove his buggy. Riding beside Francis was Father DuPontavice on his horse. Shortly before 11:00 a.m., a tall, stout Potawatomi man entered the store.

Rantz recognized him as Shabonee. Shabonee was upset because he had not received a gift in exchange for his daughter. Francis recognized the precariousness of the situation and not wanting the wedding to unravel because of his deal with Noel, quickly offered Shabonee his mule. Much to Francis's relief, Shabonee accepted the offer, but Francis sensed that Shabonee accepted the gift with a degree of reluctance. Joseph and Archange already were with Watchekee and soon led her into the store when Shabonee came to the front door and nodded his approval to them. Much to Francis's surprise, his bride was the pretty Potawatomi lady who came into Rantz's store two weeks earlier to buy 'powder medicine.'

Before the ceremony commenced, Father DuPontavice pulled a blank wedding license from his satchel. Please give me the names of the bride and groom. Francis said, "Just write down 'Francis Bergeron' for me."

When Father DuPontavice heard the name 'Watchekee,' he said while looking over his shoulder, "That won't do. The County Clerk wants a family name as well as given name!"

Watchekee quickly conferred with Joseph and Archange. She recalled that she was given the name Josette when she was baptized. However, Joseph said "Josette is a Latin name. You need an English name. How about Josephine?" Watchekee, feeling somewhat pressured at this point, agreed.

Archange added, "What is she going to do about a family name?"

"Why not just borrow ours — 'Babeu?'" offered Joseph with a shrug of his shoulders.

Father DuPontavice accepted what he heard and entered Watchekee's name as 'Josephine Babeu' on the wedding license that he planned carry to the Will County Courthouse the next day. "By the way, it would be better if there two witnesses. Right now only Mr. Duncan is the sole witness. Mr. Babeu, please be the second witness," said Father DuPontavice just before he started the wedding ceremony.

5 – Zozzette, Josette — Etta

Francis lay snoring next to Watchekee in her wigwam the morning after their wedding. She woke up having been aroused by the alarm calls of blue jays and wrens that were flitting about the branches of the nearby shagbark hickory tree and scolding a lethargic black rat snake whose escape was slowed down by the season's chilly evening. Clearing her mind, Watchekee looked over at the virtual stranger with whom she had slept. She felt very confused by the events during and following her 'white man' wedding.

Watchekee turned away from Francis and gazed at a point blanket next to the side wall of her wigwam. Underneath the blanket was the money bag that Noel had thrown at her in his store when he told her to forget about him. Reaching over and pulling the bag to her, Watchekee felt tempted to leave. *"Where?"* she thought. *"Perhaps I can buy a ride on a stage coach and go to the Illinois River. There, I can get on one of those large canoes that someone once called a paddle-wheeler and ride on it to Ft. Leavenworth or even as far as Council Bluffs. No, I need to stay with my husband even if I don't know him. Hopefully, he will be good to me and help me take care of Olivie and little Archange."*

The unique sound of a mule's loud bugle-like bray woke up Francis. First, he thought, *"Jack needs his breakfast."* As he felt the warmth of Watchekee's body next to his, he rubbed his eyes and remembered that he gave Jack to Shabonee.

Turning and looking at Watchekee, he and said, "Isn't it strange. We are married, but I don't even know what to call you. I heard you talking to Joseph and Archange just before our wedding. They called you Watchekee but you said your baptized name was something like Zozzette. Guess that you were saying Josette. But Father DuPontavice wrote your name as Josephine. Josephine, Zozzette, Josette — can I call you Etta? It's short for Josette."

"Yes, if you want to," said Watchekee as she looked over at Francis.

"Etta, then it is!" said Francis as he reached for his bride's hand.

Jack's distinct voice cancelled any amorous thoughts as Shabonee removed the hobbles that had kept Jack close to the hunting village. Etta and Francis heard Shabonee mutter, "I've never heard such a noisy beast!" Shabonee then led Jack over to the entrance of his daughter's wigwam and tied him to it.

"What's that mean?" asked Francis as he looked at Etta when he heard the rustling of Jack being tied up.

Etta started laughing. "My father gave Jack back to you. I should be insulted, but I'm not. He thinks that Jack will not be good for hunting. He's too noisy!"

Just then, two hungry girls came into the wigwam where Etta and Francis had spent their first night together. Squirming under the blankets of fur that were covering their mother and new step- father, Olivie and Archange said almost in unison, "I'm hungry!"

Etta and Francis were humored by the innocent intrusion of the hungry girls and began laughing. The girls squealed when Francis first tickled Archange, then Olivie.

Etta, who at that moment realized that Francis was going to be a good father for her daughters, said, "Alright! Alright! Let us get dressed, and I'll come and get you something to eat. Scamper! Olivie, take Archange with you and stay by the cooking fire that I smell. Be careful! We'll be out in a moment."

Etta and Francis soon fed Olivie and Archange. Others in the hunting camp were packing as if to leave. "What's happening?" inquired Francis as he looked at Etta.

She said with a sense of sadness in her voice, "Everyone is getting ready to go back to Council Buffs. The hunting is good here, but it is time for them to go back and get the winter village ready. They will go when my father returns from hunting."

"Are you — I mean, are we going too?" questioned Francis.

"No," responded Etta. "Besides, I don't want to go back — at least not right now. Anyway, I'd rather go to Ft. Leavenworth."

"Where's that? Why?" asked Francis.

Etta briefly looked at Francis and said in a recalling way, "Ft. Leavenworth? It's in Kansas. I grew up in a Potawatomi village along the Pickamick River. The village that I remember as a child is not far from here." She indicated the direction of her former village by pointing southeast with pursed lips. "Anyway, my people were removed from there about eight years ago. I have aunties and uncles who used to live there. They went to Ft. Leavenworth and are living with the Kickapoo. I know some of them too. The Kickapoo there are from Danville — a place south of where I lived as a child. I lived there once too." As if coming out of a trance, she asked Francis, "Where are you from?"

"Saint Hyacinthe, near Montreal," he responded. "It's in Canada — south of the St. Lawrence River."

"I've heard of the St. Lawrence River," Etta said.

Francis was going to ask her how she knew, but he suddenly remembered that he needed to get to work. Quickly finishing his breakfast, he said, "I've got to get to Rantz's. Glad that we have Jack. I won't have to walk! I'll be back before sundown."

"He's a good man. Someday he will find out about the father of Olivie and Archange. Should I tell him myself?" thought Etta as she watched Francis disappear down the trail

that wound through the woods north of the Kankakee River and led to the wagon road between Wilmington and Bourbonnais Grove.

6 – No More Hurt

The first few weeks went very romantically for Etta and Francis Bergeron, a Gallic or French-Canadian as he preferred. They continued to live in Etta's wigwam even though morning frosts were becoming common. Then, in mid-October, Etta's moods became unpredictable and her disposition almost intolerable. Nothing that Francis did for her was satisfactory. Consequently, he spent less and less time at home. In fact, he would see that Etta had enough fire wood each day and then vanish after saying good-bye to the girls.

During the time of Etta's unpredictability, Joseph and Archange came to welcome Noel's latest French-Canadian immigrants at a place becoming known as 'Noel's holding pen.' They could not help noting that a few Bergeron's had arrived with the new immigrants. Noel reminded each family that their moving expenses were covered by him in exchange for their services for a period of one year.

Travelling home in their buggy, Joseph said to Archange "Let's stop by Rantz's and see if Francis is in. Bet that he doesn't know that more of his cousins are in the area. Joseph pulled up his buggy and tied the horse's reins to the hitching post that Francis recently built in front of Rantz's store. He helped Archange down from the buggy and escorted her into the store. Francis was in the back of the store and did not see his friends enter. Joseph signaled Rantz who was standing behind the counter to be quiet so he could surprise Francis. Rantz and Archange smiled as Joseph stealthily crept up on Francis who was engrossed in his work.

"*Bonjour!*" exclaimed Joseph.

Francis jerked, just as expected. He immediately

recognized Joseph and began to greet and talk to him in French even though he knew that Joseph increasingly spoke English at the expense of his fluent French and Potawatomi.

Joseph stopped Francis and said, "Let's use English."

Francis, in a pleading way, said "Joseph, I need some advice. Etta — Watchekee to you — has changed. Can we go outside and talk? Please come too, Archange. What you know about Etta might help me."

The large elm tree next to Rantz's store already had lost its leaves. Normally, the shade under this tree served as a place where many social and political issues were discussed by the settlers who came to Rantz's store. However, Francis did not want to be bothered by the late afternoon's sun rays so he moved the benches from the elm to a large sugar maple that was adorned with its yellow and red leaves of mid-October.

Sitting down, Joseph asked, "What's happening, Francis?"

"Wish I knew," replied Francis. "It might have something to do with her daughters, Olivie and Archange. I keep hearing their names spoken in hushed tones around here." He glanced at Joseph's wife and said, "I know they aren't talking about you when I hear 'Archange'." Then Francis turned and looked at the ground and continued, "Sometimes the names 'Will' and 'Elihu' come up. Is something going on that I don't know?"

"What do you know about Olivie and little Archange?" asked Joseph as he tilted his head and focused on Francis.

"I figure that their father was killed in some kind of battle or raid," replied Francis. "It's not really my business so I never asked Etta about it. Some day she will tell me about it. Maybe that's what bothering her."

Joseph was quiet for a minute and then turned toward Archange who slightly nodded her head as if to say "go ahead and tell him."

Joseph started talking about Watchekee's background,

"Francis, Watchekee's beauty and her sweet nature have been — like the Bible says — a mill stone around her neck. Gurdon Hubbard was her first husband— you know — a husband in the old way. They had an infant daughter who died. A few years later, she became Noel's wife." Joseph saw a puzzled look come over the face of Francis, whose brow furrows deepened, and felt led to ask, "Didn't you ever suspect that Olivie and Archange were Noel's?"

"No," replied Francis as he leaned forward and put his head between his hands.

"The oldest boy, Elihu, is an orphan. Watchekee and Noel took him in. Noel is sending him and Will to …."

Francis interrupted Joseph, "You said 'Will!' Is he one of Watchekee's children?"

At this point, Archange said, "Will is Mesawkequa's son."

"*Me* who?" queried Francis sarcastically.

"Mesawkequa," answered Archange. "She is Watchekee's sister. Will is Watchekee's nephew, but she raised him like he's her own. It's the Potawatomi way."

As Francis heard more details about Watchekee and why she came back to Bourbonnais Grove, he began realizing why Noel was so eager to get her out of his life and use him to do so.

Archange continued by saying, "Francis, you need to know that Watchekee deeply loves you. She is afraid that if you found out the things that Joseph and me have told you — you would leave her. She has been hurt so much and has gone through so much that she doesn't want any more hurt. All of the things that Joseph and me have said are true, but there is one more thing you need to know. It should come from Watchekee, but I will tell you."

"What's that?" asked Francis who was deep in thought.

A wide grin on Archange's face caught Francis off guard considering all the things that he had just heard.

Leaning forward and putting her hand on Francis's shoulder, she softly said, "Congratulations, daddy. Watchekee's going to have a baby — yours."

Tears welled up in Francis's eyes. Staring at Archange he slowly asked, "How'd you know?"

"She told me last week when we saw her," said Archange still grinning.

7 – Kickapoo Village

Etta and Francis stood in the chill of the morning air, a chill accented by the night's frost. Olivie snuggled against her mother's leg in an effort to stay warm. Francis held little Archange in his arms. Jack grazed along the border of the wagon road that paralleled the Kankakee River and ran to Wilmington. He nonchalantly disregarded the frost that covered the grass. Etta and her children were waiting for the Butterfield Stage Coach that would start them on their way to far distant Ft. Leavenworth, Kansas. Francis was with his family to tell them good-bye and to let them know that he would be waiting for them to return.

Etta and Francis talked for several hours, well into the evening after Francis visited with Joseph and Archange under the sugar maple tree at Rantz's store. It was a good talk that resulted in a mutual agreement: Etta would visit her friends and Potawatomi relatives at Ft. Leavenworth just as she desired and, after the baby was born, would return. Meanwhile, Francis would stay in Illinois, work and find suitable living quarters for his growing family.

"Here it comes!" shouted Olivie. She was the first to spot the stage coach when it rounded a distant curve in the road.

Everybody in the Bergeron family stepped back from the road and waved their arms to signal the driver of the fast moving stage coach.

Seeing his passengers, the driver pulled on the reins of his team and applied the coach's brakes. Jack casually looked up when the coach's team stopped and stomped in front of him and the waiting Bergeron's.

Francis threw Etta's two bags to the top of the coach where the driver's assistant secured them. He didn't want them falling off should the coach hit a bump. Satisfied with what the assistant did, Francis then helped Olivie and Archange into the stage coach. After Etta told the driver where she and the children were going, Francis started to pay. When Francis reached up to the driver, Etta gently pushed his arm aside. She took a gold piece out of a bag that she was holding and asked the driver, "Will this be enough?" The driver looked at the coin that was handed to him. With a look of amazement, he turned his face aside and spit out a stream of tobacco juice. "Yep!" he said.

The moment of departure had come. Warmly embracing each other, Etta and Francis kissed and said their good-byes. Etta reminded Francis that in the Potawatomi language there isn't a good-bye — only a "until we see each other again" — *Bama pi*. Nevertheless, Etta and her daughters soon were on their way. Francis stood alone watching the stage coach until it disappeared around the next bend in the road. As long as he could see her, Olivie hung out the stage coach's window waving at him. "*Bama pi*," Francis softly said to himself. He then mounted Jack and silently rode to Robert Duncan's farm to pick up any eggs that Robert wanted to sell.

How Olivie and Archange were able to fall asleep so fast in the jostling and swaying stage coach was a mystery to Etta. Because of her pregnancy, the same motions made her nauseated. Nevertheless, she and her daughter were headed to the northern-most terminus of the steamboat lines that plied the waterways on the Illinois River. Etta quickly surmised her passage back to her people was going to be much easier and faster than going eastward thanks to the money that Noel threw at her.

Etta's stage coach arrived at the Princeton terminus later the same day as she left Francis near Bourbonnais Grove.

She was able to get a room in nearby Princeton for the overnight stay after being told that there would not be a paddle-wheeler leaving for St. Louis until morning. Etta fell asleep without eating. In so doing, she left her daughters to fend for themselves; but resourceful Olivie took over the motherly duties of caring for her younger sister quite well. Soon, all three travelers were asleep snuggled together and slept soundly through the night.

When Etta woke up early the next morning, she saw two pairs of brown eyes staring at her. She knew what Olivie and Archange wanted. Knowing that the S.S. Argonaut was not scheduled to leave until 8:30 in the morning, Etta was able to get breakfast for her daughters. After one bite of the biscuits and gravy, Etta pushed her plate aside. Picking up her bags, she then hustled Olivie and Archange to the loading dock and boarded the waiting S.S. Argonaut that already was belching out its ominous columns of black smoke and blowing its horn to announce its imminent departure.

Archange turned to her mother as they were scurrying up the gangplank and asked when the paddle-wheeler blasted its loud horn, "Is Jack here?

A one-day layover in St. Louis gave Etta time to reflect on the time she came through the area when she was a follower of Kennekuk, the Kickapoo Prophet. Late in the afternoon, she crossed paths with Major Hitchcock, the army officer who took her back to Council Bluffs less than a year ago. *"He's the one who called me an indigent Indian,"* recalled Etta. *"I'd like to say something to him, but he'd probably send me back again although I doubt if he'd remember me."*

When Etta got up the next morning, she hurriedly took Olivie and little Archange down to the riverfront. There she got tickets for herself and her daughters on the S.S. Rosebud, a paddle-wheeler destined for Council Bluffs although, as planned, she would disembark at the Ft. Leavenworth landing.

It took Etta just two weeks to reach Ft. Leavenworth after she said farewell to Francis along the road northwest of Bourbonnais Grove. Her trip west was much easier and faster than the one by horseback from Council Bluffs to her former home along the Kankakee River in northeastern Illinois. She marveled at the scenes afforded by the numerous waterfowl that she viewed from the decks of paddle-wheelers as they belched smoke and made their rhythmic, churning sounds whether going down the Illinois River or up the Mississippi and Missouri rivers. Etta previously never had had the opportunity or luxury to enjoy her travels. Only emotional traumatic flashbacks of her past life interfered with the marvels she was now experiencing.

Etta's whole body was filled with excitement when she first set foot on the landing at Ft. Leavenworth. She looked up at the oak trees that bordered the landing, but soon became anxious to see her old friends and relatives who had left the Pickamick River village in 1832. There were other friends that she wanted to see in the Kickapoo village also. They had come to Ft. Leavenworth about the same time as the Potawatomi after spending a few years in Missouri. Etta knew some of them from the time that she lived in Danville, Illinois, with Hubbard. She had been given to him by her uncle, Tamin, who wanted to secure trader-Indian business relations. She shuddered and thought, *"Glad that Francis and I got a 'white man' wedding."*

8 – Uncle Sid

Francis spent the next several months glum and somewhat depressed. He continued candling eggs, which were becoming increasingly scarce as the weather became cold, and mashing corn but did so silently. Rantz found it hard, if not impossible, to engage Francis in conversation. One day in mid-March, Francis came in, stomped the wet snow off his boots and told Rantz, "I'm out of work until the corn crop is harvested next summer. Besides there are more pressing matters, so you won't be seeing me for awhile."

"Oh! What's that?" asked Rantz as he wiped his hands on his shirt and walked out from behind the counter is his store so that he could talk more directly to Francis.

"I miss Etta and the girls. Besides it isn't right that she is going to have her baby, and I'm not with her. She went to a place called Ft. Leavenworth. Know it?

"Yeah. It's along the Missouri River several miles north of a place they call Westport. That's about all I know."

"I'll find it. Will have to ask along the way, but I'll find it."

"Good luck."

"Also, I told Etta that I'd find a better place for us and the children to live than in her wigwam. Also told her that I'd find work, you know, work to better support her and the family. I was supposed to do this while she was gone, but haven't been able to do either yet."

Another man was leaning up against the counter idly talking to Rantz when Francis came. It was Sid Vail, a long-time friend of Rantz, who politely stood back to let Francis talk to Rantz.

After Francis got through talking, Rantz introduced the two men, "Francis, this is Sid Vail or 'Uncle Sid' as he is better known. Uncle Sid this is Francis Bergeron. Francis has been candling eggs and mashing corn for me. He's also done other odd jobs for me."

"Glad to meet you, Francis" said Sid, initiating a hand shake.

"Same here, Uncle Sid."

"You're looking for work and a place for your family, eh? I overheard you talking to Rantz." Sid slightly turned to Rantz as he said this. "What's your wife's name? Take it you got some children? How many?"

Uncle Sid's questions were coming faster than Francis could answer them. Finally, Francis said, "My wife is Etta. Some around here better know her as Watchekee."

"Watchekee? Thought she went to Council Bluffs awhile back. Wasn't she ....?" Sid stopped his question when he suddenly realized that he was going to enter a sensitive subject. Before Francis could respond, Sid said, "Want some work? I need someone to split some rails and do some fencing for me. My neighbor gets tired of my bull coming over to see his cows. I'm tired to having to chase him back home." He winked at Rantz and added, "The bull that is. I also have an empty cabin. It's a two-room cabin with a 'dog trot' alleyway down the middle that separates the two rooms. Can't pay much but can let you and your family live in the cabin. I live over by Momence — the other side of Bourbonnais Grove."

Francis graciously thanked Uncle Sid and said, "I won't be able to start until I get back from Ft. Leavenworth next summer."

"Whenever! Rantz can help you find my place."

Uncle Sid and Francis shook hands again as they left Rantz's store at the same time. Uncle Sid climbed into his buggy and headed southeast to Bourbonnais Grove where he would turn east towards Momence. Francis mounted Jack and said, "Let's find Etta!"

Francis, bundled in a heavy coat and fur hat, started plodding in the same direction that Etta and the girls took when they left on the stage coach five months earlier. Then it was mid-October when lower temperatures were just starting. It was mid-March now, and winter had not yet broken its icy grip along the Kankakee River Valley.

Knowing that Etta had boarded a paddle-wheeler at the Princeton terminus for her trip to Fort Leavenworth, Francis decided to do the same thing. After all, he still had some of the money that Noel had given to him and could pay for his passage. He hoped that the Illinois River would be free of ice. "Jack, glad we had a mild winter," he muttered, but Francis didn't know if he could take Jack aboard with him. "*If necessary,*" Francis thought, "*I'll sell you when I get to the landing.*"

9 – Goin' to Join My Wife

Jack started his bugle-like braying when the S.S. Delaware began blowing its horn. First, his vocal eruption startled nearly everyone on the loading dock. Then people, passengers and workmen, alike started laughing at the echo-type concert that ensued.

Francis saw the workers scurrying, some rolling large barrels and others with carts loaded with miscellaneous cargo. There were several groups of passengers waiting for the gangplank to be lowered so they could board. Francis asked what appeared to be a workman, "Where can I buy a ticket?" "At the ticket office!" was the curt reply. "Better hurry, the boat leaves in ten minutes!"

Francis rode Jack over to the ticket window, got off his mule and inquired, "Does this boat go to Fort Leavenworth?" He rudely was informed that the boat only went to St. Louis and that he would have to find another boat going to the Kansas Territory. "Can I take my mule?" he next asked and was much relieved to discover that livestock could be taken but at a price.

After getting his ticket and paying for Jack, Francis walked back to the landing dock leading Jack. He then realized that he wasn't seeing any other passengers. "Hurry up! Yes, you over there!" Suddenly, Francis realized that the command was aimed at him. He pulled at Jack's reins, but the mule balked at going across the gangplank. "Try riding that beast across!" shouted a crew member standing on the upper deck. "We are going to leave any minute!" Just then, the horn of the S.S. Delaware sounded. Jack let out his bugle-like bray again, and Francis kicked him in the flanks. Fortunately, the strategy worked although Jack bucked and lurched his way across the gangplank and onto the deck. Francis, wide-eyed, simply slid off Jack and was much relieved that he was firmly on his feet on the deck of the paddle-wheeler and not in the icy waters of the Illinois River. The people who saw him dismount began applauding and cheering.

Following the directions of a laughing crew member, Francis led Jack to a small, roped off area that served as a corral on the boat's stern. "Jack, we're headed for St. Louis," said Francis sitting down to catch his breath. He did not feel the cold wind and was unconcerned about the ice floes that were floating down the river.

"Glad that you made it! This boat barely made it up from St. Louis yesterday. From what I know, it is making the first round-trip of the season. Where are you headed?" spoke a friendly passenger.

Francis looked up and meekly said, "Ft. Leavenworth."

"Ft. Leavenworth, huh? You'll have to transfer in St. Louis and probably again in Westport — Westport, Missouri, that is. By the way, I'm Isaac — Isaac McCoy. My home's in Westport. I've been in Michigan visiting some of my Potawatomi friends. Not many of them left in these areas, you know." Pausing and looking at the river, he offered, "If you need any help, just let me know."

"Thanks! I'm Francis Bergeron by the way."

Isaac turned and started walking away, but pausing and turning slightly back to where Francis was sitting asked, "Hope you don't mind, but what takes you up to Ft. Leavenworth?"

"I'm goin' to join my wife, Etta."

"The husband going to join his wife? Usually I hear that the wife is going to join her husband."

"Well she left a few months ago to be with her people on the Kickapoo Indian reservation when our baby comes."

"She must be Kickapoo then."

"No! She's got some Kickapoo friends, but she's Potawatomi."

"Potawatomi! What's her name?" asked Isaac as he grew more intrigued whent he heard Francis say."Etta."

"Etta? That's not a Potawatomi name!"

"Etta's her nickname. Her baptized name is Josette."

"That makes sense, but you must know her Potawatomi name."

Francis, moving his legs and shifting his sitting position to be more comfortable said, "Watchekee." As he spoke he was distracted by a large flock of geese gliding and landing on the river next to the far bank.

"Watchekee — Watchekee. Don't think that I ever met her, but seems that I have heard of her. Most of the Potawatomi that I know came from Michigan and Indiana."

"You say 'came.' What do you mean by that?"

"It's a long story. Back to your wife. Do you happen to know her mother or father —. or their names?"

"I met her father, Shabonee." Francis stuck his thumb backward at Jack and said with a slight chuckle, "Tried to give him my mule here for my wife, but he gave him back. Etta said that her father didn't like him."

"Shabonee! I know who he is. Never met him either, but heard that he once was with Tecumseh. He helped carry Tecumseh's body to a place east of Detroit — Wahpole Island if I'm not mistaken — after the Indians got beat at Thames, Ontario. He later warned white settlers around here that the Sac and Fox were causing trouble. It didn't set very well, even with some of his own people. Know where he's at now?"

"Just a few months ago he was near Bourbonnais Grove along the Kankakee River, but he should be back in western Iowa by now."

Pulling his coat around him, Isaac who was starting to shiver asked, "Can we talk more later? I need to get out of this cold wind."

"Gladly!" said Francis as he stood up. He then looked back at Jack to make certain that he had hay and water. He then strolled off to seek his own relief from the wind.

10 – Emerging From the Wigwam

Ice floes drifting down in the current of the Missouri River slowed the ascent of the S.S. Bishop as it made its way from St. Louis to Westport. It was at this juncture that the river made nearly a right angle bend and continued northward. Francis would not know until he got there if the river was still open and if river boats were operating to Ft. Leavenworth. Francis already decided that he could ride Jack the remaining thirty-five miles if necessary.

The trip that Francis was undertaking gave him ample opportunity to learn more Potawatomi history from Isaac. Isaac explained that there were several removals of the Potawatomi from the Great Lakes states and territories. The one that he was most familiar with was the forced removal of Menominee and nearly nine hundred others from northern Indiana two years earlier. Isaac frequently referred to them as the Mission Band. Francis learned the Potawatomi on that removal lost a large number of people, mostly the young and elderly, and were taken to east central Kansas.

Isaac was very comfortable calling these Potawatomi the Mission Band because he was a pastor who once ran the Carey Mission. It was near the St. Joseph River, a significant water way that flowed through Indiana and into the Michigan Territory. Isaac was Baptist and not comfortable when discussing the influence that Father Benjamin Petit, a Jesuit missionary priest, had on these Potawatomi. His interest in talking to Francis suddenly waned when Francis informed him that both he and Etta were Roman Catholics.

There was reason for Francis to be concerned for his personal safety when he arrived at Westport. Two days before, a paddle-wheeler churning up the Missouri River had to turn back before reaching the Ft. Leavenworth Landing because of the large number of trees that were being brought down the river with the melting ice floes. The boat captain said that it was too dangerous.

Much to the surprise of Francis, the captain of the S.S. Bishop announced that he would continue going up river after unloading the boat's cargo and getting a fresh supply of wood for the boat's boilers at Westport. Francis went to check on the condition of Jack. While brushing his mule, he said, "Jack, we've made it this far. Let's hope we make it the rest of way to find Etta and the girls."

The trip from Westport to Ft. Leavenworth went slower than usual because of the choked waterway, but the captain of the S.S. Bishop carefully and skillfully navigated the paddle-wheeler up that stretch of the Missouri River. To have done otherwise, the captain might have collided with a sawyer and sunk his vessel. The arrival of the S.S. Bishop was the first of the season. Upon its docking, there was much jubilation on the loading dock from a handful of soldiers from the nearby military installation and several civilians.

Francis was relieved when he reached the Ft. Leavenworth landing. He quickly saddled and bridled Jack and led him down the gang plank. Fortunately, his getting off the S.S. Bishop lacked the acrobatic gyrations of his getting aboard the S.S. Delaware nineteen days earlier.

Before leaving the river front, Francis asked a worker who was busy rolling a barrel of flour, "Which way to the Kickapoo?" The worker scarcely looked up and hastily pointed north. He said, as he spit a stream of tobacco juice, "That way, about five miles."

The information that Francis got surprised him because once he got to Ft. Leavenworth he mistakenly thought he would be able to quickly find Etta. Considering the day's lateness, Francis decided to find a livery for Jack, get a room in a nearby tavern for himself and ride to Kickapoo Village in the morning. Between the bed bugs and his anxiety, Francis had a long, sleepless night and hardly could wait for the sun to rise. He hoped he could get to the village before noon.

The wagon road to the Kickapoo Reservation wound across several bluffs overlooking the Missouri River and through ravines marked by yet dormant oak, hackberry and black walnut trees. *"This area is very scenic,"* thought Francis. Caught up in his thoughts high on one of the bluffs, Francis began smelling smoke. Soon, he saw several plumes of smoke rising from the valley that lay ahead of him.

The Kickapoo village that Francis was about to enter was comprised of the Kickapoo, who dominated, and the Potawatomi, who had come from the Pickamick River in northeast Illinois. The Kickapoo as a whole were very much opposed to any intrusion from the white man's world and were very independent even internally. Those who remained on the Ft. Leavenworth Reservation largely were followers of the Kickapoo Prophet, Kennekuk. Etta formerly was one of his adherents, but her main draw to the area was the presence of the Potawatomi who were there. After all, she grew up with them until her mother, Monashki, under the orders of Tamin, gave her away to Hubbard, a trader, when she was only fourteen or fifteen years old. The Potawatomi on the Ft. Leavenworth Reservation could offer her the solace and comfort that she needed as she waited the birth of her child.

Francis was intrigued by the number of elm bark-covered wigwams that he saw as he entered the village. Men were returning with deer from their morning hunts, and women were involved with a sundry of chores near the entrances to their wigwams. Each dwelling's entrance had a single doorway that led outside to an overhanging roof. In front of it was a table about the wigwam's width. Francis thought, *"Etta and me lived in one of these at Bourbonnais Grove."* Because the village's inhabitants were warily watching him with benign glances, Francis felt he might as well have been an invisible ghost.

As Francis slowly rode through the village, he spotted two young girls who were helping an elderly woman carry wood to a cooking fire near a distant wigwam. The older girl was Olivie. She happened to look up. When she did and saw Francis sitting atop Jack, she exclaimed, "Father!" Her shout caused Archange and the elderly woman to look in the direction of the stranger. They stood motionless as Olivie dropped her armload of wood and ran to Francis. Francis jumped off his mule and swept Olivie off her feet amidst Olivie's squeals of joy. Just then an obviously pregnant woman appeared in the wigwam's entrance carrying an empty water gourd. She was Etta who stared in disbelief when she saw who was in the trail. First, Etta held the gourd tightly, but then dropped it when Francis lowered Olivie to the ground and started walking and then running toward her.

An elderly Potawatomi man followed Etta out the wigwam. Thinking Francis was an unwelcome intruder, he quickly got in front of Etta. Before Etta could stop her grandfather, he unsheathed his knife and lunged at Francis. Deftly, Francis jumped sideways and avoided a stabbing or slashing. Etta screamed, "Stop! It's Francis!" The elderly man suddenly realized his mistake and went and stood by his wife who was the elderly woman carrying a load of wood. Wide-eyed, Olivie and Archange watched as their mother and father embraced. Etta and Francis each had taken a long trip to reach this point of tenderness.

They once again stood united. Suddenly, their moment of bliss was shattered by the trumpet-like blare of Jack's bray when he saw a horse in the distance. Francis and Etta only could laugh at the moment of broken silence as they held out their arms, signaling Olivie and Archange to join them.

11 – Them Half-Breeds?

Next to their elm bark-covered wigwam, Olivie and Archange played with a warty toad they caught in the woods on the Kickapoo Indian Reservation north of Ft. Leavenworth. It was early June, and the warm rays of the late spring sun filtered through the ample leaves of a nearby sycamore tree. Francis nervously paced back and forth, looking at the innocence of his carefree daughters, while he waited for Etta to birth their child. Although in the pain of labor, Etta's mind flashed back to the rough conditions she faced in Princeton, Illinois when Archange was born only three years earlier.

After hearing a moan, Francis heard Etta's grandmother say in her muted voice, "You got a son!" She avoided calling Francis by name because of her inability to pronounce "r's."

Francis sheathed his knife, dropped the stick he was whittling and entered the wigwam he and Etta shared with her grandparents. Taking a few moments for his eyes to adjust to the dimness of the wigwam, Francis blinked his eyes and saw Etta lying on her willow bed that was padded with a trade blanket. Etta, although her face was covered with perspiration, beamed at Francis. Snuggled next to her was their newborn son. Francis tried to remain stoic but his misty eyes told Etta otherwise. Finally, he grinned broadly, leaned over and kissed her cheek.

Ten days passed when Etta said, "Francis, we still haven't named our son."

"I've been thinking of a name that has some of his French family history. He will grow up knowing the Potawatomi culture, but still should have a name that will remind him of his French heritage too."

"I was born on a night that something unusual happened so I was named Watchekee and became an overseer of my people's history. What is the name that you've been thinking about?"

"John Baptiste."

Two weeks after the birth of John Baptiste, the family of now five was on the loading dock at Ft. Leavenworth. Francis wanted to sell Jack to pay for the river boat passage for his family back to Illinois. However, Etta was opposed to the idea of Francis parting with his mule. Anyway, she had grown to like Jack. Opening up a small bag, she took out two gold pieces and said, "Francis, I think this will be enough for all of us, including Jack, to get back and have John Baptiste baptized. We could go up to the mission at Council Bluffs but I would rather that Father DuPontavice do the baptizing. He's still at St. Michael's in Joliet isn't he?"

"Yes! As far as I know. We could go directly there, but let's first find Joseph and Archange. Bet that they'll let us stay with them for a few days. We can then get John Baptiste baptized. Afterwards, we can go to the Bourbonnais Grove area and find Sid Vail. He actually lives near Momence, east of Bourbonnais Grove. I told you that he offered me a job and us a place to live when we get back. I met him at Rantz's."

"You've been thinking alot. Joseph and Archange shouldn't be too hard to find," replied Etta. "Archange has a reservation at Skunk Grove. It's not far east of Joliet."

"Huh! How'd she get a reservation?"

"Her father was an important fur trader, and he got her written into a treaty. That's how."

"Say! Where did you get all your gold? Did you sell a reservation?"

Etta simply said, "No." Her mind suddenly drifted to the life she formerly had with Noel and Mesawkequa and the last painful conversation she had with Noel.

Francis saw a look of hurt come across Etta's face and thought to himself, *"I'd better leave well enough alone. Maybe someday she will explain how she got her bag of gold."*

"It's amazing!" Francis said to Etta as they were getting off the S.S. Carrie V. Kountz at the Princeton landing dock. The terminus near the confluence of the Illinois and Vermillion rivers was the same place that each had separately departed for Kansas several months earlier. "We left Ft. Leavenworth only twelve days ago. It helps to be going down the Missouri most of the way."

"Yes!" said Etta. "Also, there weren't many trees floating down the river either. — Olivie! Take Archange's hand!"

Etta and Francis were aware as they got off the S.S. Carrie V. Kountz that rocky rapids just upstream prevented their steam boat from navigating any closer to where they were going. Carriage transportation seemed the most viable option so Francis left his family standing on the loading dock and rode Jack to the local livery barn. There he bought a buggy, two carriage horses, and the necessary tack for the horses to be harnessed and hitched to the buggy. After buying an axe in the hardware store next to the livery barn, Francis tied Jack behind the buggy and went back to the loading dock to get his waiting family.

Once everyone was loaded, they started heading in the direction of Joliet following the Illinois River. "Oh, untie him! Won't he follow us?" commented Etta with a slight chuckle in her voice soon after leaving town. Francis responded with a slight shrug of his shoulders, stopped the buggy, got out and untied Jack.

"You better," whispered Francis into Jack's ear.

The Kickapoo village in Kansas seemed a distant past as the family drove across the northern Illinois prairie. Etta imagined the time when the Kickapoo and her own people, on horses, chased buffalo across the prairie. *"Now,"* she thought, *"they're not here. My father told me that he remembered seeing buffalo and elk in his childhood."* She then paused and said almost as speaking to herself, "We're gone too — at least most of us."

"What?" asked Francis as he drove the team.

Jack tended to get distracted by the prairie grasses and lollygagged behind to dine on them. Olivie was given the responsibility of keeping track of him. Each time she was about tell her mother that Jack was missing, a blaring trumpet-like bray signaled that Jack was coming and would soon catch up with the buggy.

Being told at the livery that the distance to Joliet was about 80 miles, Francis figured buggy travel would take four or five days and planned on camping when they stopped each night.

Because of Etta's knowledge of the prairies, Francis depended on her to choose their camp sites. Each site was on the edge of the Illinois River Valley, just inside the edge of the woods. She chose such locations as a precaution should a lightning strike set the prairie ablaze. She wanted a place where they could retreat if it became necessary to do so.

Upon stopping as evening approached, Etta and the girls unhitched the carriage horses and took them and Jack to a bordering sandbar along the Illinois River to drink. "Watch Archange!" Etta cautioned Olivie every time they stopped. "Don't let her get in the current of the river!"

Francis shot game from the forested areas for the evening meals. While he was hunting, Etta, Olivie and Archange hobbled the carriage horses so they could graze for the night and then set up camp. Willow branches were cut with the axe that Francis bought after disembarking from the river boat and bundled into sheaths. The bundles were stacked against the sides of the carriage to provide some protection should it rain. Etta's primary concern during the carriage trip was keeping John Baptiste and her daughters dry.

Upon hearing the sounds of the muzzle loader, Etta knew that the firewood that she and the girls had gathered would soon be used to cook supper. Usually, Francis came back carrying a raccoon and a squirrel or two. Francis did the skinning and cleaning. After Etta finished suckling John Baptiste, she turned to cook the fresh game. Meanwhile, John Baptiste was oblivious to the whole routine as he slept contentedly in the cradle board strapped to Etta's back.

Etta began recognizing more landmarks the closer they got to Joliet. Travelling past Joliet, Francis stopped when he saw a settler riding his way in hopes of getting directions to Joseph's and Archange's cabin. After all, he and Etta wanted their close friends to be their son's godparents.

"Afternoon, sir" said Francis. "Do you happen to know Joseph Babeu and how we can get to his place?"

"You mean them half-breeds?" was the gruff reply. "They's two miles down the road in Skunk Grove." Just as he spoke, he looked at Etta and into the faces of Olivie and Archange who were sitting in the back seat of the carriage holding their baby brother. "Sorry," the man half-heartedly said and rode off.

Silence pervaded the carriage until Skunk Grove came into view. Both Francis and Etta had been dwelling on the man's attitude. "Francis, I hope that Joseph and Archange are home," said Etta rather hesitatingly. After a few minutes, she perked up when she saw a cabin. Etta put her hand on the shoulder of Francis and excitedly said, "There they are! That's them working beside the cabin!"

12 – Kankakee River Valley

Following the baptism of John Baptiste by Father DuPontavice in St. Michael's Church in Joliet, Francis and Etta drove south to Bourbonnais Grove to find Sid Vail. Francis planned on driving to Rantz's store because he knew that Rantz could tell him how to find 'Uncle' Sid. The only route passed through Bourbonnais Grove, right past Noel's house. It was early Sunday afternoon when Francis and Etta arrived at Bourbonnais Grove. As they drove into the village, Francis recognized Rantz's horse. It was hitched in front of Noel's house.

"We're in luck!" said Francis. "We won't have to drive out to Rantz's. He's here in town, and we can get directions here." Francis stopped the carriage and hitched his team next to Rantz's horse. He started for the door of Noel's house but noticed that Etta had turned her back as if to say, "Don't." Seeing Etta's body language, Francis returned and climbed back into the carriage. Picking up the reins and leaning forward, he quietly said, "We'll wait for Rantz to come out."

Twenty minutes passed before Rantz appeared in the doorway. He was followed by Noel. They shook hands and were starting to say good-bye when Noel saw who was in the carriage. He abruptly ended his conversation with Rantz and went back inside.

Rantz was rather perplexed by Noel's sudden change in demeanor. Looking to see what caught Noel's attention, Rantz was greatly surprised to see Francis and Etta sitting quietly in their carriage. Their three children were asleep in the back seat. Jack was standing nearby. Rantz hurried to carriage to greet Francis and Etta. After several minutes, Francis got general directions to Sid Vail's house. He and Etta then thanked Rantz, said good-bye to him and drove to Momence to find 'Uncle' Sid.

Francis reined in his team when he saw a man standing beside the wagon road that ran between Bourbonnais Grove and Momence. His purpose in stopping was to ask the man if he knew how to find Sid Vail. The man gave Francis a sullen look as if to say that he didn't understand. Etta quickly intervened. "He's Potawatomi. Let me talk to him." Potawatomi was a language that Francis was learning to go with his repertoire of French and English, but he was not sufficiently fluent enough to use it in such situations.

Etta had a short conversation with the Potawatomi man, who smiled with his eyes when he heard Sid Vail's name mentioned. Without looking at Etta, he turned and pointed east with his lips. He then started walking down the wagon road, opposite the direction that Francis and Etta were traveling.

"What did he say?" asked Francis.

"We're almost there, but we need to turn east when we come to a large oak tree and follow a road up to a white house with a picket fence around it."

A two-story white house came into view just after Francis and Etta came over a slight hill. After turning they were on a road that resembled more of a lane than one of the public wagon roads that were becoming increasingly common in the area as more and more white settlers moved into the Kankakee River Valley. Nevertheless, it led right into the front yard of Sid Vail's residence.

A spotted coon hound's baying alerted Sid to the arrival of visitors. As Francis and Etta drove into the yard, Sid opened his front door and stood on the front porch to see who had come.

Recognizing Francis, Sid walked down the porch's

steps and to the carriage.

"Greetings, Francis. I haven't seen you since we met at Rantz's." Looking at Etta, who was cradling John Baptiste, and the two girls, he politely said, "Must be your family. Glad to meet you, madam."

Sid's next comments were a great relief to Francis. "Still looking for work? I've got plenty for you to do, and the cabin in the woods still's needin' a family to live in it."

"Yes, indeed," responded Francis who looked at Etta and could see that she was pleased at what she had heard.

Etta was marveling at Sid's house when a diminutive lady came out of the house and approached her and Francis.

"Oh!" said Sid. "Please meet my sister, Phoebe — Phoebe Johnson. She and her husband, Leland, live in Momence. She stopped by for a visit. Phoebe — necksFrancis here will be working for me. He and Mrs. Bergeron and their family will be movn' into the log cabin."

"Welcome!" chirped Phoebe.

"Say, Francis, when do you want to start?" asked Sid.

"How 'bout tomorrow if we can move into the cabin yet today?"

"Sounds good!"

Phoebe was getting ready to drive her one-horse buggy back to Momence, but paused momentarily and said, "Oh! I see that you've got a newborn! Mrs. Bergeron, you must be exhausted! Bless your heart! Let Sid know if you need any help and I'll come out from Momence"

"Thank you," replied Etta.

****

Early the next morning, Francis awakened to the sound of axes and falling trees. He rubbed his eyes, ran his fingers through his hair and went outside. Three men already were at work in the timbers behind the log cabin that he and Etta had moved into.

Francis went back inside and aroused Etta. He hoped that she could at least brew him some coffee before he joined the other men. Etta did as he wished and breast-fed John Baptiste at the same time. She not only made coffee for Francis but cooked him some of the eggs and salt bacon that Uncle Sid had given to her when he showed the cabin to her and Francis. Francis thought to himself, *"I don't know how she does it."*

His thoughts then turned to the work that 'Uncle' Sid wanted him to do, *"Sid must have a lot of work to do."* As soon as Francis ate his breakfast, he finished getting dressed and hurried outside to join the men who were felling timber. He was delighted to learn that all three were Potawatomi. To his amazement, the men not only spoke their tribal language but French and English as well. Working side by side, Francis and the other workers cut down black locust trees and split them into rails for Sid's corn field and orchard.

Francis was astounded but pleased to know there were Potawatomi still living in the Kankakee River Valley. He discovered the workers and their families basically had sought refuge in the Beaver Lake area and the Kankakee marsh of adjacent Indiana. The friendship Sid Vail had established with the Potawatomi living in the vicinity was well known.

Over the next few years, the working relation between Francis and Sid got to the point where Francis became Sid's partner. Etta and Phoebe simply became friends, strong and lasting friends.

13 – Purple Mist

Francis finished the second cultivation of the corn and thought, "*Just one more time and the corn'll be too tall to cultivate again this year.*" Tired and dirty from working in the field, he led his sweaty team to the barn. There, he unharnessed his horses, Babe and Blackie. As soon as their bridles were removed, they broke for the horse tank outside the barn. Francis watched as the horses quivered their flanks and stomped their hooves to dislodge the pesky flies that swarmed about them. After slurping their fill of water, Babe, followed by Blackie, flopped on her back and rolled back and forth in an area void of any vegetation. Francis laughed to himself when he saw the cloud of dust that was created. The frolicking provided each horse with a layer of dirt to discourage the flies and a rewarding scratch for a day of hard labor.

Seeing that Francis was in from the field, Etta got a bucket of fresh water from the well and took it to him. Ladling the water, Francis quenched his own thirst, looked at Etta and gave her a smile of appreciation. Francis, leaning against the split rail corral that he and his co-workers had built the previous year, began chatting with Etta about the peacefulness they were enjoying. As they talked, they watched Olivie and Archange tromp through the cabin yard after having fed the chickens. At the same time, John Baptiste came toddling out the log cabin searching for his mother.

While Francis and Etta were savoring this moment of relaxation and watching the innocence of their children, Sid came driving down the lane. He was returning from Momence where he had gone to take care of some banking. Sid hitched his carriage horse in front of his house and walked over to

Francis and Etta. Both Francis and Etta could tell by the look on Sid's face that he had something serious to tell them.

Francis listened in disbelief to what Sid told him. Etta, though a strong woman, broke down sobbing. Their tranquility and peacefulness and that of their children were soon to end.

According to the 1832 Treaty of Camp Tippecanoe, all land held by the Potawatomi living in the Kankakee River Valley was ceded. This treaty, coupled with Indian Removal Act of 1830, decreed that all eastern Indians were to be removed to lands west of the Mississippi River. Although, the remaining Potawatomi in the area had lived peacefully with their new white neighbors, they still were told they had to leave.

Sid wanted nothing to do with the removal of the Potawatomi whom he had befriended. Etta was torn. She wanted to stay, but she and all the other Potawatomi were told otherwise. Francis was confused and angry. He did not want his family to be torn apart. Politics and the financial interests of realtors were in favor of the increasing white population, not the Potawatomi.

****

Several Potawatomi, some in tears, sadly came by to say good-by to their friends, 'Uncle' Sid and his family. Seeing that the Potawatomi had accepted their fate, Sid agreed to help conduct their removal. He wanted to make certain that they were treated kindly, unlike some of the early removals from the Chicago region that he had heard about.

Shortly after noon in mid-June, Francis finished loading his oxen-drawn wagon and looked longingly at Etta. She stood expressionless by the log cabin holding John Baptiste. With her free arm, she huddled her daughters next to her. Francis finally asked Etta, "Are you ready?" She said nothing as she helped Olivie, Archange, and John Baptiste get into the horse-drawn carriage. Slowly, the oxen and horses began moving down the lane. Etta drove the carriage, and Francis, astride Jack, led the oxen. They planned to join the rest of the removal in

Bourbonnais Grove.

It was late in the evening before Francis and Etta made it to Bourbonnais Grove. Much to their surprise, familiar voices were heard, "We heard that you're going to Council Bluffs. Can Archange and me join you?" Their friends, Joseph and Archange, from Skunk Grove had arrived..

"Archange, I thought you could stay because you were given a reservation," said Etta in a curious but pleasing voice. Archange answered rather sadly, "Joseph and me always got called 'half-breeds' and didn't get along with the neighbors so we're goin' back too. Joseph and me can come back to Skunk Grove someday — if we want to. I still got it."

The main body of the removal came into Bourbonnais Grove and set up camp near the Kankakee River. It was a strange mixture of horse- and ox-drawn wagons, some loaded with personal possessions and others with families. Other people were walking as their dogs trotted in front of them.

Sid made a special effort to find Francis and Etta. They were preparing their evening meal when he spotted them. Riding up, he dismounted and asked, "Can I camp with you tonight?"

As darkness descended, numerous camp fires glowed along the Kankakee River. Their flickering flames brought peacefulness but belied the sadness felt by the Potawatomi who were being thrown out of their homeland. While staring into the camp fire of Francis and Etta, Sid told of one of the most heart wrenching things he had seen so far, "While we were crossing the Kankakee River, there were so many people splashing through the water that the mist looked purple. It was the color of the setting sun. One blind woman was clutching onto the blanket of a young girl in front of her. The girl started across the river. I saw the blind woman hesitate when she felt water on her feet. Yet, she followed the young girl not knowing what might be next."

The following morning, the removal party lacked a sense of organization. Finally, Sid got everyone lined up and told them that they should start moving when he waved his arm. Before he could get the wagons going, Noel unexpectedly came riding into camp. He sought out Francis and Etta. After an animated conversation with them, he tied his horse to the back of Etta's carriage, climbed into the front seat, and took the reins. Etta quickly got into the rear seat and pulled her children to her side.

"Why are you doing this?" asked Etta with sharpness in her voice.

"Olivie's my daughter and you said Archange's mine too." After a long pause, Noel said, "Ruth told me that I should help you and Francis. You know that I sent Elihu and Will to school. Do you want me to help support Olivie and Archange?"

"No thanks! Francis and me will raise them. We're doing quite well. This removal is hard on us, but we'll work things out just fine."

The first day there was not any more conversation between Etta and Noel or any between Francis and Noel. That evening as he did the rest of the time that he was on the removal, Noel joined Sid.

As the second day unfolded, Etta began telling Noel what she had done since he threw her out. "I soon found out that I was pregnant and had Archange during the 1837 Removal. Later, I was even called an indigent," she said. When Noel heard Etta talk about these and other ordeals, he began to fully realize his error.

Noel remained silent and there was no outward indication that he could do anything to rectify the matter. The closest thing was what he said earlier back in Bourbonnais Grove: "You know that I sent Elihu and Will to school. Do you want me to help support Olivie and Archange?"

During the next several days, Francis and Etta engaged Noel on a variety of conversational but insignificant subjects. All the while, Noel felt very uncomfortable. When the Mississippi River was being ferry-crossed, he untied his horse from Etta's carriage and stood aside. Etta then got in front and drove her carriage onto the deck of the waiting ferry. Once she and Francis were both aboard, Noel simply mounted his horse and started back to Bourbonnais Grove.

14 – Quito's Reply

Etta's returned to Council Bluffs as a family woman with substantial wealth, the amount unknown. She no longer was an indigent, but she felt she was an outsider even among her own people. The reason was partially due to her dressing like her white sisters rather than in the feminine Potawatomi clothing of the day. Her choice of attire stemmed from her social interactions with the Vail's over the past three years near Momence, Illinois.

Growing up, Etta lived in the Potawatomi world as Watchekee. Then her life shifted to the trader's world after her uncle and mother shoved her into it. Etta's worlds kept changing afterwards — Kickapoo — trader — Potawatomi — farmer's wife — once again Potawatomi. She looked forward to finding solace in St. Joseph's Mission in Council Bluffs, the mission where she and her daughters were baptized.

When Etta and Francis arrived at the mission that was a short distance east of Trader's Point next to Steam Boat Landing on the Missouri River, Francis wrinkled his brow and said, "I thought you said we were going to a mission. This place doesn't look like a church. It looks like a fort!"

Laughing, Etta replied, "It used to be a fort. Some dragoons, you know, soldiers, built it several years ago. Then it was given to Billy Caldwell. He let Fathers DeSmet and Verreydt use part of it as a mission. Olivie and Archange were baptized here. Later I was too. Father Verreydt baptized me. He's the one who gave me the name 'Josette.'"

While Etta and Francis were standing in front of the stockade-style mission an elderly Potawatomi man came walking by them with down cast eyes. "Excuse me," said Etta in Potawatomi. "Do you know if Billy Caldwell is around? What about Fathers DeSmet and Verreydt? I can't find any of them!"

The answer shocked her: "Billy Caldwell died two years ago. Cholera! No more mission here. Fathers left."

Etta was hoping to see some familiar faces.

Francis saw the shocked look on her face. "Perhaps we should go to the Indian Agent and get some more information," he said in effort to calm Etta.

"The agent lives on the other side of the river. That's where the agency is. I've gone there to get annuity payments for me and my children."

"How can we get across the river?"

"A ferry crosses it. We'll have to go south along the river for a couple of miles. We can get on there. You'll see the agency across the river when we get on the ferry."

****

Francis looked around the agency grounds while Etta went into the Agency House to talk to the Indian Agent. Etta recognized him from the times that she came to get her annuities and from the time that she was sent from Ft. Leavenworth as an indigent who belonged at Council Bluffs.

The Indian Agent was Edward James, a bearded but bald-headed man whom William Clark, the co-leader of the Lewis and Clark Expedition that explored the Louisiana Purchase, had hand-picked. What little hair remained on Mr. James's head told Etta that it once had been reddish. Because of his bald pallet, the Potawatomi gave him a name when translated into English meant 'Stone Sticking Out Of Water.' Mr. James thought that he was given an honorable name but Etta remembered that men in Shabonee's village snickered whenever the Indian Agent's Potawatomi name was spoken.

Etta started to tell 'Stone Sticking Out Of Water' that

she and three children were sent to the Council Bluffs Agency from Kankakee.

"Yes! Yes! I know. Several hundred of you arrived yesterday!" he said curtly. The manner in which he spoke made Etta feel uncomfortable. "What's your name?" Mr. James asked as if talking to a stranger.

"Etta — uh, Josette Bergeron," she replied haltingly.

"No! No! Your Indian name. You must be Potawatomi since you came from Illinois, but there are Odawa and Ojibwa here too."

"You might have me on the rolls as Watchekee. I've been here before. Look under the Potawatomi who are enrolled."

The Indian Agent looked up at Etta. He vaguely remembered her, "*She looks like one of them that Major Hitchcock brought in from Ft. Leavenworth a couple of winters ago. One of them indigents. Yes! One of them indigents —. but she can't be!*"

Francis knew that Etta did not want to settle on the east side of the river especially when she was told that her father no longer was in the area. He had returned to his little reservation in northern Illinois. Walking into the Agency House with his three children by his side, Francis sensed that Etta and the agent were just about finished.

Mr. James looked up and peered through his glasses. He asked, "Are you Watchekee's husband?"

Francis nodded and politely said, "Yes."

"She can't be," softly muttered 'Stone Sticking Out Of Water' after Etta and Francis left his office. He then turned to his aide and said, "We've got more important business to deal with than knowing where she came — yesterday or whenever. According to this communication from Ft. Leavenworth, Major Wharton will be here next week. He's coming to talk about uniting the Potawatomi here with the Osage Sub-Agency bunch. The War Department wants all the Potawatomi on the same reservation. Guess that it's gonna be somewhere in Kansas. Whose Major Wharton gonna talk to? Caldwell's dead, Shabonee went back to Illinois, and old Wabaunsee is in Washington City talking with President Van Buren."

"Don't know," replied the aide. "How 'bout Big Foot?"

"Naw! He's too cantankerous. Besides, he won't talk to nobody! Quito just came up from Kickapoo Village. He's a little feeble but might be well enough to meet with the Major."

****

Francis searched around and found a job getting supplies that came in by paddle-wheeler and driving them to the Sub-Agency. It wasn't a full-time job, but the work led Etta and him to live in Nebraska near the Sub-Agency. He was gone when Etta saw and talked to Quito and several other men heading for the Agency House.

The encounter with Quito was a pleasant surprise to Etta. She knew him as a respected elder from the Pickamick River as well as from the short time that she lived in Kickapoo Village. Quito's presence in Council Bluffs was comforting to Etta.

When Quito entered the Agency House, he saw Major Wharton sitting behind a small oak table. Next to him was Edward James, the Indian Agent. An empty, straight-back chair was positioned on the other side of the table. It obviously had been placed there for Quito.

Quito glanced at the men who had accompanied him, the empty chair and at Major Wharton who then invited Quito to sit. He did so by opening his hand and slightly gesturing toward the chair. Quito did not move, but continued to stare at the Major.

Finally, Major Wharton cleared his throat and, through the aid of a translator, began explaining the purpose of his coming to the Council Bluffs Reservation.

Quito continued to stare at Major Wharton. He suddenly interrupted the translator in the English tongue, "I know why you are here, Major. We Potawatomi feel like we are birds caught in a windstorm. The boughs keep moving, and we don't know which one to land on."

Major Wharton sat dumfounded and his face flushed.

Quito firmly said, "When a Potawatomi has something important to say, he stands — not sits." Seeing that he caught Major Wharton off guard, Quito added, "I learned English at the Carey Mission in Michigan." With that remark, he whirled and left, followed by the men who had come with him.

15 – Her Fate

The splashing of horse hooves in the watery mud along the east bank of the Missouri River and the whiny of horses were heard on a sunny day in September 1846. The sounds were a precursor of what happened one year later. Wagons loaded with people and their meager possessions packed the ferry across from the hill on which the Agency House stood. Dogs on the ferry ran back and forth, barking incessantly. A few wagons remained on the bank. They would load onto the ferry when it returned. Potawatomi men who were mounted plunged their horses into the river, herding rider-less horses in front of them, when the ferry started moving westward. The congestion occurred down river below Trader's Point.

Despite Quito's blunt but eloquent talk with Major Wharton, his words of reality were coming true. Although the Potawatomi leaders had signed a treaty in the summer of 1846, the government had in effect caused another windstorm and left many Potawatomi wondering what branch of the tree they would land on next.

Etta and Francis had heard rumors from various sources about the Potawatomi at Council Buffs moving to Kansas. They overheard soldiers at the fort talk about what might happen. Some of the notions came from the workmen on the loading dock at Trader's Point. Now, because the relocation actually had started, Etta and Francis could no longer dismiss the rumors.

****

Etta and Francis had grown accustomed to the

surroundings of Council Bluffs where they were comfortably rearing their family. Their livelihood came from raising chickens and hogs, which they supplemented with produce from their vegetable garden. Any extra poultry and hog products readily were sold to the commissary at the nearby fort.

On the day that Etta and Francis saw the start of the move to Kansas, they were sitting outside their log cabin watching their children play. Olivie was now ten years old, Archange, eight, and John Baptiste, whom the girls nicknamed 'Bat,' five. The newest member of their family, Matilda, was eleven months old.

Olivie and Archange were playing with faceless corn husk and thrum dolls that Etta had made for them. Bat was poking a long willow stick at the chickens that were strutting about the yard, scratching up grubs and snatching grasshoppers. Matilda was not walking yet but reveled at being able to pull herself up and accomplishing a teetering stand. It was at this moment of joy that the Indian Agent stopped by under the pretense of a friendly visit.

"Morning, Francis. You too, Mrs. Bergeron." James tipped his hat as he acknowledged Etta and unconcernedly exposed his bald head. His shiny head immediately reminded Etta of his Potawatomi name. "You have some fine looking children." He then cleared his throat and said, "Say, I have some important information. You know, the chiefs signed a treaty with the government a few weeks ago. The Council Bluffs Sub-Agency is being eliminated. All Potawatomi are being moved to Kansas and united with the people from the Osage Sub-Agency. Some people already have started moving."

"Yes! We saw them," said Francis with a look of worry starting to come across his face. "What does this all have to do with us?"

"Mrs. Bergeron is Potawatomi. Your wife and your

children received annuity payments last year. I let you pick up their money because she was expecting. Remember?"

"Of course" said Francis who by this time was standing a few feet from James. "What does the move to Kansas have to do with us?" When he asked his last question, he looked over at Etta who looked back at him. Francis then shot his gaze directly at James.

James could not look at Francis and said almost inaudibly, "Mrs. Bergeron has to go too." Pausing and taking a deep breath, he said, "Your children too. You don't have to go for two years." Showing no regret, 'Stone Sticking Out Of Water' climbed back on his horse and rode back to the Agency House.

Francis stared in disbelief at the vanishing Indian Agent. Turning to Etta who was standing and holding Matilda tightly to her, he muttered recalling what he had heard Quito say to Major Wharton, "What branch does he think we will land on?"

Etta and Francis quietly walked into the cooking side of their dog-trot cabin. Matilda, who had outgrown her cradle board, rode on her mother's hip. Francis poured coffee into this white, enamel cup and sat down. His thoughts were entirely consumed with the disruption that his life and that of his family soon would be facing. *"James didn't say nothing about me,"* he thought. *"Don't suppose he thought I would not go?"* Looking out the window next to the kitchen table, he saw three of his children playing with their dog. It had just come home after a futile morning of chasing cottontails. *"Glad they are happy and don't know nothing."*

Etta moved over to see what Francis was watching. Seeing the children, she put her hand on his shoulder and asked, "When do you think we'll move?"

Francis remained quiet for several minutes. Finally, he dejectedly said, "Next year about this time. We'll want to get the crops in. I want us to have enough food to get us through the first winter in Kansas."

Resigned to her fate, Etta dropped her arm and walked over to the fire place where a black pot was bubbling with beans and pork. A pan of sweet potatoes rested on the hot coals below. "Want something to eat?" she asked.

"Yeah," answered Francis as he bounced Matilda on his knee and looked out the window at his other children. His mind flooded with the memories of the events that he and Etta had shared since they got married in Bourbonnais Grove. "*Love in spite of an arranged marriage — getting together again at Kickapoo Village — births of John Baptiste and Matilda— the friendships of the Vail's — removal to Council Bluffs — struggle to survive in Council Bluffs — tranquility — what next?*" Etta knew that Francis was deep in thought and left him alone.

16 – Possible Attack

    The main body of the Council Bluffs Potawatomi made its way across the Missouri River and the exodus to the new reservation in Kansas in the fall of 1847. The wagon road that the Potawatomi took passed by the log cabin where Etta and Francis had been living for the past three years. Archange and Olivie looked up from where they were playing with their faceless dolls. The girls saw countless wagons loaded with people, possessions, supplies, and basic camping gear approaching them.
    There was a mixture of dress among the Potawatomi. Most of the full bloods were dressed in traditional clothing. Diversifying the clothing were the half-breeds and the few white husbands who wore the clothing of the dominant race that was poised to fill the vacuum of the departing Potawatomi.
    Some wagons were pulled with oxen, others by horses. Willow-branch cages, holding chickens, tied to the sides of a few of the wagons looked like ornaments. Small herds of pigs were herded by men and older boys with long sticks. Dogs with their tongues hanging out trotted beside the wagons. There were many horses herded by young men riding bareback.
    Suddenly, it was a race between the two sisters to see who could alert their parents first.
    Francis, upon being excitedly told of the approaching wagons, looked at Etta and asked, "Are we all packed and ready? She scarcely nodded and looked longingly at the log cabin. Etta remembered the many happy times she and her family had in it. Seeing the moving mass of people and

animals, she took Matilda by the hand and yelled to Olivie, Archange, and Bat, "Get in the back of the wagon!" Francis already was on Jack and leading one of the milk cows. The other cow was tied to the back of Etta's wagon. When an opening presented itself, Etta and Francis fell into the line and headed south to Kansas.

Young children in the departing Potawatomi were stimulated by the moving line with all its smells and sights. They showed much excitement. Many of their parents and grandparents were remorseful. Having to move from their homes and villages in the Council Bluffs area reminded them of the sadness and hardships of being removed from the Great Lakes region a few years earlier. Once again, they thought, *"What tree branch will we land on in the ever blowing storm?"*

One day before reaching the Kansas River, Francis tied his cow to the back of Etta's wagon and rode to the front of the procession to discuss where the group might camp for the evening. Any thoughts of where to camp suddenly became secondary to what the men were about to hear. First, Francis and the others saw a distant cloud of dust. Then, two riders came into view. Both men were holding the reins of a trailing horse. It was obvious that the men were riding hard. Those watching the incoming riders knew the purpose of a spare horse. It could be mounted should the lead horse bearing the weight of a rider drop from exhaustion.

The leaders of the group that Francis had gone to see were relieved to see that the two men were friends who left Council Bluffs one year earlier. The leader told the sweaty and dust-covered riders that they were more than happy to be able to join their brethren south of the Kansas River. However, everybody became very concerned when the two riders said why they had come: POSSIBLE ATTACK BY A WAR PARTY FROM AN UNFRIENDLY TRIBE!

Francis didn't go back to guard Etta and their children until scouts chosen from the blue moiety (firstborns) were sent out to look for any war party that might be intent on attacking.

Joseph Babeu and his wife, Archange, were trailing several wagons behind the one being driven by Etta. Like Francis, Joseph was riding beside Archange's wagon; but he was dozing as his horse clopped along when the alarm call sounded. Immediately, Joseph became alert, heeled his horse and quickly rode up to Francis for information. After conferring with Francis, Joseph quickly whirled his horse around and re-took his position beside Archange. This time, he was fully awake.

"What's wrong?" asked Archange with a slight tremble in her voice.

"Watch for anything that looks like a war party!" replied Joseph who raised his voice in order to be heard over the sounds of the turning, steel-rimmed wheels as they crunched on the wagon road and the squeaking axles.

"War party? I thought we were too far south of the Yankton Sioux!"

"Francis told me that a war party from a tribe in the Rocky Mountains might attack. Just be alert! We're still going to stop tonight! We're not too far from Ft. Leavenworth and can get help if necessary. However, guards will be posted for safety. We should be able to reach the Kansas River about noon tomorrow. We'll be safe there!"

All the men in the wagon train took defensive precautions as they checked their guns and powder horns. Still others strung their bows and readied the arrows in them. The women forgot about the sadness they had borne ever since leaving their homes in the Loess Hills of western Iowa. Everything became a mode for survival.

The sight of young Matilda whose jowls jiggled in cadence of the jostling wagon caused Francis to be even more concerned and surfaced the memory of the time that Etta had told him that she was pregnant: *"I was excited about going to Trader's Point to get supplies for the Agency that day. There was a big shipment from Westport on a paddle-wheeler. Freeze-ups had prevented any river traffic for several months. Our supplies were really down.*

Dampness made the trip very cold. Even my buffalo coat and hat didn't keep me from shivering. I got home late, but Etta got me a warm dinner. The children were spinning tops by the fireplace. They were the tops that I had whittled for their Christmas presents.

I remember stripping off my bulky coat and hat and standing by the fire and rubbing my hands to warm them up. I was still stomping my feet when I looked down at the children and said to Etta, 'They are growing up fast. I think we should have another baby one of these days. Etta grinned broadly and told me, 'You won't have to wait long.' Her eyes twinkled in the flickering light from the fireplace.

I stopped rubbing my hand hands and couldn't believe what Etta had just said. 'What? Are you sure? When?' I picked up Etta and spun her around. The children, wondering what was happening, looked up and stared at us.

Etta said, 'I think the baby will come in October.'"

****

"What's happening?" implored Father Hoecken to himself when he saw the arrival of the Council Bluffs Potawatomi. He had ministered to many of the Potawatomi from the Osage Sub-agency in Kansas and had moved with them. He clearly saw that both groups of Potawatomi were jubilant when they saw each other. Relatives and friends were being reunited after many years of being separated. However, Father Hoecken could not understand why the reunion was south of the river. After all, the new reservation was north of the river.

Father Hoecken wandered about the clusters of people next to their camp fires and was heartened by what he heard.

The people were catching up on the news of their family members and friends after so many years of being forcibly separated. Interspersed with the laughter and crying were discussions of what the Potawatomi were going to do now that they were together. Still, Father Hoecken was baffled by where the Potawatomi had gathered. As he wandered about the dancing and talking groups, he spotted Francis who was looking at a log structure.

"Good evening, sir," said Father Hoecken.

Surprised to hear Belgium-accented English and the black robe of a priest, Francis spun around and said, "Oh! Hello, Father."

Francis put out his hand to initiate a handshake and to introduce himself. "By the way, I'm Francis Bergeron," he said.

"Father Hoecken," was the reply.

Continuing to engage Father Hoecken in conversation, Francis asked curiously, "Is this a mission I'm looking at? The cabin looks like the chapel."

"Yes! This is a mission, and you are looking at the chapel," said the Father with a sense of pride. "I recently built everything here with the help of the Potawatomi from the Sugar Creek Mission near the Osage Sub-agency. I wanted to set up the mission north of the river, but was told that if I wanted any help I had to build it south of the river. The creek by where you and your family were eating this evening, I named Mission Creek. Still can't understand why the Potawatomi wanted the site for the new mission to be south of the Kansas River."

Francis said, "I think I know."

17 – Cross Creek Bridge

Anticipated attacks by tribes from the west never materialized, and the Potawatomi began moving north across the Kansas River in 1848. Soon they occupied the region that the government intended to be a common reservation for the Mission Band and the Prairie Band. Before Etta and Francis moved from the Mission Creek area, Etta requested one thing of Father Hoecken. She made the request on one of her frequent trips to the chapel. Part of her draw to the Mission was she overheard Father Hoecken mention to Francis that he came from St. Ferdinand's Church in Florissant to minister to the Potawatomi.

Late January, Father Hoecken was startled when Etta quietly walked up to him. He was chopping down an oak tree to be used as a log to help expand the mission at the time.

"Yes?" he asked. "May I help you?"

"I was wondering if you know Fathers DeSmet and Verreydt?" Etta replied as she tightly clutched her capote for warmth. Just as winter set in she had made her capote from an old point blanket that she and Francis had brought with them from Illinois.

Putting down his axe, Father Hoecken said, "Yes! We all came from St. Ferdinand's Church. It's in Florissant, Missouri, down river from here — near St. Louis." With a slightly cocked head, he asked rhetorically, "Why do you ask?"

He knew that the two priests Etta inquired about had been sent from St. Ferdinand's to establish a mission at Council Bluffs. What surprised Father Hoecken is that his colleagues were involved in the baptisms of Etta and her daughters.

Father Hoecken was starting to shiver but listened patiently as Etta told him why she really wanted to talk to him, "By the time I returned to Council Bluffs in 1843, both Fathers were gone, and there was no mission. Matilda, my youngest daughter, was born two Octobers ago and still hasn't been baptized. I want her baptized soon. When can she get baptized?"

"I understand your situation. First, I need some information. Has Francis been baptized? How about John Baptiste? "

"Yes, both have. My husband was baptized in Saint Hyacinthe, Quebec, you know, Canada. My son John Baptiste — uh, we call him Bat — by Father DuPontavice in Joliet, Illinois."

Father Hoecken laughed, "Bat? How did he get that name?"

"His sisters," answered Etta with a slight grin.

"Let's set a date. I know!" said Father Hoecken. "Pierre Dyoyard and Angelique Wawaiatinokmet are getting married two days from now. I know that Francis will be one of the witnesses. Want to have Matilda baptized after the wedding?"

Because of Etta's growing faith in Roman Catholicism, she was pleased in knowing that Matilda was going to be baptized. It was a sacrament that had eluded her in Council Bluffs. Jubilant, Etta hurried home to tell Francis.

****

"Father!" Archange screamed. She was watching two-year old Matilda trying to catch spring azure butterflies that were sitting and flying about a mud puddle when Francis suddenly tumbled out of sight. He had been on a steep bank above Cross Creek, a tributary of the Kansas River into which it flowed southward.

Etta looked up. She, Olivie and Bat were nearby picking tender milkweed leafs for supper. It would be part of their first meal in the log cabin that Francis and his friends had just finished near Cross Creek.

Alerted by her daughter's scream, Etta dropped her bucket and ran over to the spot where she last saw Francis. She could see that a portion of the creek's bank had given way. Peering over the edge of the embankment, she saw Francis sprawled in mud among rocks and facing upward. He appeared lifeless. Etta's heart pounded, and she put her hands to her mouth in disbelief to what just happened!

Francis then opened his eyes and started laughing.

"What? Are you hurt?" asked Etta who had been distraught one minute, now relieved but confused and becoming perturbed.

"I was looking for a place to build a bridge across the creek!" shouted Francis still laughing. "I found it!"

"I don't care about no bridge! Are you hurt?" asked Etta as she slid down the steep bank of Cross Creek to reach Francis. Cradling Francis in her lap and arms, Etta asked Francis again, "Are you hurt?"

Francis looked up at the edge of the embankment and saw four pairs of brown eyes staring down at him and four mouths aghast. In order to relieve everyone's concern, Francis slowly got up on one elbow and sat up. Turning to Etta, he said with a sheepish grin, "I didn't move after I landed in the mud 'cause if something was broke it would hurt."

"You!" said Etta. "Let me help you up!" Wiping dirt and mud off Francis while they were climbing up the bank she asked, "What do you mean 'build a bridge'?"

"I heard that the mission's gonna be moved to Miami's village west of us. We'd have to ford the creek each time. Others gonna have the same problem. The creek's too small for a ferry, and its banks are too steep for fording it. We need a bridge. I talked to Tescier and Lawton yesterday. They said they'd help me build one. I was looking for a good spot to build it when I fell."

A few years after the bridge was built, Francis discovered that his milk cows were gone. A section of the split rail fence that he had built was down. The cows' hoof prints led in the direction of the bridge where they intermingled with several wagon wheel tracks. "Etta!" Francis hollered. "Bring me my gun! I'm going after our cows!" Etta appeared in the cabin doorway and handed Francis his gun, but she was not quite sure of what was happening. Francis quickly bridled up Jack, leaped onto his back without bothering to saddle him and thundered across the bridge.

Two miles down the trail, Francis was amazed to see Louis Vieux herding his two milk cows in his direction. "Hello!" said Louis when he and Francis met. "I was coming to see you this morning about your bridge. About a mile back I came across a wagon train. You know, some of them white people going to a place called Oregon. A fellow on one of the wagons stopped me. He pointed to your cows and asked me if I knew who owned them. He noticed them after crossing your bridge. I said, 'Yeah, I know the owner. I'll take them to him.' Didn't tell him that I was planning see you anyway."

Francis said "Thanks. Thought they got stolen. Glad I didn't have to use this." He lifted his gun a few inches that he was holding across the withers of Jack. "What about my bridge?"

18 – White Man's Politics

Blood and violence. These words best describe Kansas shortly after Etta and Francis moved there from Council Bluffs although they sought only tranquility.

The pursuit of Kansas statehood took three political paths. One was championed by Isaac McCoy before the Potawatomi came down from Council Bluffs. He wanted Kansas to become a state for Indians governed by Indians. His idea actually preceded the formation of a common Potawatomi Reservation. An act on this matter passed in the U.S. House of Representatives but was tabled in the U.S. Senate. Eventually, the effort never came to light again in Congress. The other two ideas caused considerable tumult. Was Kansas to be a free state or one that allowed slavery?

Several weeks after Francis got his milk cows back, he and Louis, shaded by an enormous elm tree, talked about a bridge that Louis wanted built across the Vermillion River. Their discussion took place several miles west of where Etta and Francis lived near Cross Creek. Francis and Louis seemingly were unaware of what was happening politically in the territory or didn't care. Francis listened intently to what Louis said, "Francis, hundreds of wagon come this way each day. It's become known as the Oregon Trail. When they get here, they quickly forget about the high price of forage that the Potawatomi there charge them back at the new mission, St. Mary's. The big problem here is getting across the Vermillion. It's something they have to do if they want to keep going." Smiling he added, "I figure they wouldn't mind paying a toll rather than risk going down the steep banks and getting stuck in the river or get killed trying." Little did

Francis know that the bridge or at least the era in which it was built and operated was to become the entrée to a somewhat mixed period in the lives of Etta and himself.

Upon returning home near Cross Creek one day later, Etta and Francis had their own discussion after their meager evening meal of beans, stewed raccoon and milkweed leaves. It was frank.

"You said that you were going to see Louis about building him a bridge. Now you start talkin' about workin' for him after the bridge is done!" exclaimed Etta. "What kind of work? His bridge will go over the Vermillion River." Etta became emotional and shouted as she turned and pointed westward, "It's there!" Spinning around to face Francis again, she said in a calculated voice, "We're here!"

Francis knew that Etta would be easier to reason with in the morning and tried to go to sleep without responding to her concerns. However, deep sleep seemed to avoid him. He tossed and turned instead. Over and over, his mind played out the events of recent years and how they surely must have emotionally affected Etta. *"The senseless death of Magdalene. Etta still is in grief. She wants to take the blame, but I put her on the ground to play. I didn't see the copper head. We now have Catherine but almost didn't. Etta's pregnancy was hard on her. Then Catherine came too early. We had to keep her warm by the fireplace. It was a real struggle keeping her alive for the first few weeks after she was born."*

Francis arose the next morning and tried to quietly slip out the cabin without disturbing anyone. As he headed for the milk shed, Jack spotted him and trumpeted his bray. The mule's loud call in turn set in motion the combative squeals of three hogs fighting over places in their slop trough.

Grimacing at the racket, Francis turned and saw Etta grinning and standing in the doorway of the cabin. She was holding Catherine. One by one, other pairs of eyes peered out the door. Seeing the innocent faces of his children, Francis walked to the cabin porch. There he held out his arms and brought everyone to him.

He took Catherine in one arm and embraced Etta with the other. While doing this, he said to Etta, "Louis wants to hire me to help him run the bridge. It's gonna be a toll bridge. I need a job so I can take care of you and the children. A new village, Louisville, is being built not too far from where the bridge will be. Also, St. Mary's Mission, the new mission's name, is just a few miles east of the village. It's starting a school. We can send the children there so they can learn to read and write."

Etta looked around and finally at her children. "Francis, me and you have been thinkin' of the same thing concerning the children. I've long wished that they could go to school. Life's been hard for us here. Back in Council Bluffs, you could get work at the fort or for the agency. Here, there's nothing!" There was a slight pause and then she said, "Tell me more about the village."

The idea of a school opening at the new mission intrigued Etta. In late 1850, she and Francis drove to the mission on what had become known as the Oregon Trail. In addition to getting information about the school, they received a pleasant surprise.

"Well hello!" greeted Etta when she unexpectedly saw her sister, Mesawkequa. "I haven't seen you since Francis and I got here. What brings you to the mission?"

"Nothing really, "replied Mesawkequa. "Just wanted to see it."

During the visit, Francis, sensing that Mesawkequa wanted to talk to Etta in private excused himself and went to find Father Hoecken.

After talking to Mesawkequa for an hour, Etta went in search of Francis. She found him talking to Father Hoecken along with a new priest, Father Duerinck, who had just arrived. After Etta was introduced to Father Duerinck, Father Hoecken explained that Father Duerinck would be living in Louisville to take care parish matters there.

Happy to hear that a priest was going to be in the Louisville area, Etta cleared her throat and apologetically said, "Francis, we need to be getting back if we want to get home by dark."

Francis looked out the window at the sun's shadows and said to Fathers Hoecken and Duerinck, "I didn't know that it was getting so late. Please excuse us, Fathers."

The buggy ride back to Cross Creek gave Francis an opportunity for him to find out what Etta found out from her sister. It didn't take long. In fact, Etta began talking about her visit with Mesawkequa before they got out of St. Mary's.

"Got some news about Elihu and Will," said Etta as she looked in the direction of the Kansas River. "Elihu and Will? Are they still in Detroit where Noel sent them to school?" replied Francis. After a long pause, Etta took a deep breath and said, "They went back to Bourbonnais Grove after a few years and worked for Noel a couple of years. Will then went to live with his father in Galena, Illinois."

"Where's Galena?" queried Francis. "Is it close to Bourbonnais Grove?"

"No, it's quite a ways from Bourbonnais Grove. It's near the big river far to the northwest," answered Etta.

"Did Elihu go with him?" questioned Francis, starting to become concerned upon learning that the two boys didn't stay in Detroit.

He became more attentive after what he heard Etta say next.

"Mesawkequa told me Elihu's living here on the reservation. He's got a place near her up Soldier Creek. Elihu went with her to Ft. Leavenworth. He said in court there that he knew her. It must've helped her sell her reservation land back in Illinois. My sister isn't the only one I talked to."

"Oh! Who else?"

"Archange and Joseph. They're going back to Skunk Grove — plan to leave next week. Things weren't workin' out for them here — I guess."

****

Wagons bearing the Bergeron's and their possessions passed over Vieux's bridge that spanned the Vermillion River on the Oregon Trail. Francis drove the lead wagon, and Olivie expertly managed the team of oxen pulling the hind wagon. Etta looked down at the river they were crossing and said, "Francis, I understand why Louis needed a bridge. You said this is a toll bridge, but we didn't have to pay anything." "I know," said Francis. "Potawatomi don't have to pay, only the white settlers."

"We passed through St. Mary's, but where's the new village?"

"You mean Louisville? It's just a couple of miles ahead."

Francis turned southwest onto the wagon road that led to Louisville. "Originally," he said to Etta, "this was a military road. It still goes to Fort Riley, but it also runs right past Louisville. Most of us around here call it the Louisville Road. Look at it! It goes to Ft. Riley, and Louisville is close to the Oregon Trail!"

Louisville offered Etta and Francis the peacefulness they had pursued ever since they were forced to leave Kankakee. Through his employment at the toll bridge and the revenue from the store that Francis opened in the growing community, financial security also was realized. Etta and Francis became land barons when they purchased ten residential lots.

One evening Etta and Francis sat down to have a quiet evening meal. It was five years after they moved to Louisville. Hearing a knock on their cabin door, Etta and Francis gave each other a surprised look. The sound of his chair scooting back from the table was insignificant on the dirt floor. The children, though famished, remained obediently quiet and still. Opening the door, Francis saw three men, all local members of the Free Soil Party. He immediately recognized them and invited them in.

"Evenin' Francis. You too, Mrs. Bergeron. Sorry to interrupt your supper," said Henry Heinecke, the spokesman for the group. "We would be greatly obliged, Francis, if you would serve as our party's election judge. The upcoming election is very important you know. It will decide the fate of our state's constitution as to whether we become a free state or one that tolerates slavery. Of course we want it to be free. Francis, we know that you are not a citizen but your filing intent to become a naturalized citizen qualifies you to vote and to serve as an election judge. You would be an election judge for District 10, here in the Rock Creek Precinct. Interested?"

"That's right. It's territorial law," piped in Aaron. "Filing an intent is all that's needed. Ain't that so, Dean?"

Dean merely nodded his head in agreement.

"I would be honored, but....," Francis started to say.

"Good!" replied Henry before Francis could say anything else.

Francis, although he felt that he had been suckered, simply asked, "What do I do?"

"Come to the courthouse. Sit and watch the voting. Afterwards, count the votes. Not many people here can count. Thanks. Evenin' Francis, and you too, Mrs. Bergeron. Thanks again, Francis."

Not showing any reaction, Francis returned to the table. After prayer was said for the meal, Etta quietly said, "You don't realize it, but you've just entered white man's politics."

19 – The Shootings

BOOM! Zing! Etta's buggy horse jumped sideways. It was startled by a loud gunshot that rang out from one of the beige, limestone hills that overlooked the eastern end of Vieux's bridge and the explosion and spray of dirt in front of it. Etta fought to control her horse. She desperately needed to prevent a run-away. It might have fallen off the bridge dragging the buggy with it and sending Etta to certain death.

Louis Vieux came running and glanced at Etta to see if she was wounded. Seeing no blood, Louis ran back to his horse. By the time he hurriedly saddled it and rode up the hill from which the shot came from, he only found horse hoof prints. The tracks showed that the shooter had galloped his horse towards St. Mary's. Seeing the futility of trying to apprehend the shooter, Louis returned to the bridge. Etta waited for Louis to return to assure him that she was not hurt. After crossing the bridge, Etta raced her buggy horse to Louisville. When she arrived, she still was shaking from the shooting incident. In addition to concern of the harm that almost came to her, her maternal instincts were sensitized because of the baby that she was carrying.

Etta was returning from the St. Mary's Mission when the shooting at the bridge occurred. She had gone to the mission after receiving word that Mesawkequa would be there. Etta was excited about going because it had been several years since last seeing her sister. However, the messenger also said that Mesawkequa needed to talk about Will. Upon hearing that, she had said to Francis, "Something's wrong!"

Etta arrived home a few minutes before Francis came in from his wheat field where he was sowing next year's crop.

Earlier in June, he had successfully harvested his crop with a McCormick Reaper. He and several of his neighbors, including the local priest, had jointly purchased the new fangled device after reading about it in the *Ohio Cultivator*.

Etta's buggy horse was sweaty and standing in front of the hitching post in front of the cabin when Francis arrived. *"Etta usually unharnesses her horse and puts it inside the pen as soon as she get home,"* thought Francis. *"She must really be in a hurry."*

Francis opened the cabin door and saw Etta. The look on her face told him that she was scared. She did not look like her usual impish and jubilant self. Etta turned toward the door when she heard it open. Seeing Francis and seeking comfort, she rushed to him and fell into his arms. "What's wrong?" Francis implored. There were several minutes of silence before Etta moved away from the security that she felt in her husband's embrace. "Someone shot at me!" said Etta somewhat hesitantly.

"What? Where?" exploded Francis. "By the bridge when I was coming back from the mission. I think that it was a warning shot. For what I don't know."

Francis was becoming incensed to think that somebody would harm his dear Etta. As he paced around the cabin, he suddenly thought, *"Suppose it has anything to do with my deepening involvement in the Free Soil Party?"*

While Etta and Francis were talking about the shooting, Catherine and Matilda, holding a wooden pail filled with un-husked black walnuts, came bursting through the open cabin door and ran almost into them. Together, the girls, sweaty and with ankles bearing countless chigger bites, asked, "When do we eat?"

Etta managed a gentle smile and said as she stepped away from Francis, "Supper will be ready when Bat comes in from the field." Then, she looked at Matilda and at the fireplace where she saw a blackened pot of stew bubbling and cooking. "Thanks, Matilda," Etta said appreciatively.

After the children crawled up to the sleeping loft in the cabin later that night, Etta told Francis about her visit with Mesawkequa, "Will is sick. The way my sister talked, he must have TB. Mesawkequa doesn't want to go see him, but wants me to. Guess she figures that I'm more like his mother than she is. After all, I raised him for several years after she left Bourbonnais Grove."

"Do you think you should go?" asked Francis.

"Perhaps, but I don't want to leave you here alone with the children. Maybe we should all go. I have been thinking about seeing my brother who lives near the St. Joseph River in Michigan. Later, we could go visit Will. I hope that I can nurse Will back to health. If I do, I'll bring him back here. I could have our baby there."

"Our *baby*?" blurted Francis.

"Shh," said Etta in a soft voice as she rolled over to Francis. "You'll wake children, especially Bat. He just climbed into the loft and went to bed. *Yes*, our baby. I'll have it next summer — about the time when blackberries are ready to be picked."

"I don't care about the blackberries. How did you get pregnant? You're over forty years old!" said Francis who stared at the ceiling in disbelief of what Etta just said.

Weary from the day's events and her 'family way,' Etta muttered as she drifted off to sleep, "Grandmas can have babies too …."

Falling asleep was difficult for Francis. His mind alternately raced with the thoughts of Etta being shot at and being told that she was pregnant. Eventually, the weariness of his field work overrode the emotions that had flooded his mind.

POW! A loud shot woke up Francis and Etta. It came from the little corral that Francis had built for their milk cow, oxen, horses and Jack. Aroused from a deep sleep, Francis frantically shouted to Etta, "Get down — on the floor!" He pushed her off the bed and onto the floor.

Half-dressed, Francis charged to the front door and grabbed his pistol. It was primed and loaded, ready to scare away cougars that occasionally but still stealthily roamed the northern end of the Flint Hills. Slowly opening the cabin door, Francis crept out in a semi-crouch. Illumination of the full moon allowed him to see. Not encountering any gunfire, he then bolted around the cabin in the direction of his livestock pen. As Francis stood beside the split rails of the pen, he made out the figure of a man running and disappearing into the tall prairie grasses that bordered the hayfield where he and Bat had worked during the day.

Francis decided against pursuing the man. He started looking at his livestock to see if he could account for all of them. Initially, the light of the moon revealed that nothing was wrong. Then, he made out Jack. His favorite riding animal was lying on the ground, not moving.

After dashing back into the cabin, Francis fumbled around to light an oil lantern. "What's wrong?" concernedly asked Etta who had armed herself with her husband's black powder gun and was guarding the ladder that led to the children's sleeping loft. "I think Jack's been shot!" yelled Francis, lighting the lantern and adjusting its wick. He then ran out of the cabin to get a better look at Jack. *"Perhaps he's just wounded!"* Francis hopefully said to himself as he opened the gate to the pen and ran to look at Jack.

Unaware the Etta had followed him and was standing beside him, Francis inaudibly said to himself, "Jack's dead." The glow of the lantern showed that he had been shot in the head. Etta handed Francis the long-barreled gun that she was holding and slumped down to her knees. She cradled Jack's still warm head in her lap. The warmth contrasted with the night's chilly air. Unlike her stoic nature, Etta began to sob silently. At first, Francis stood with his head lowered. Then he stiffened his posture, and his mind began racing. *"My involvement against slavery has put my family in danger. I need to get Etta and the children out of here!"*

****

Still trying to grasp what he had learned and happened during the night, Francis set about finding people who would take care of his livestock while he and Etta were gone. In return, he had to give his neighbors his hay and wheat crops for the coming season because he had no idea of when he would return. He only could say that he would send them a message as to when he would be back. For legal purposes, Etta had to get permission from the Indian Agent at St. Mary's for her and her children to leave the Potawatomi Reservation. After all, as American Indians, they had been declared wards of the federal government per congressional act.

Assured that his property would be cared for in his absence, Francis returned home to discuss travel and future plans with Etta. He found her sitting in the front of their cabin. She was shaded by the simple roof that extended from their cabin. She and her daughters were shucking the green and black rinds off the walnuts that Matilda and Catherine had collected the day before. A pile of discarded rinds covered their bare feet. A few un-husked black walnuts remained in the pail that Matilda and Catherine had used to collect the pungent walnuts. A small wooden bucket contained the walnuts that had been un-husked and already were turning black. When aged, their fleshy kernels would flavor cookies and bread.

Francis smiled as he saw his family working together. "Matilda, go find your brother. If he's in the field, tell him to come home. We need to make some travel plans. I think we can get ready to go about week after we get a cabin moved for Father Duerinck."

"What about the walnuts?" fussed Catherine.

"We can give them to Olivie and Archange," answered Francis who deemed the walnuts of little value considering that he was preoccupied with more serious matters. "They can have them. Besides, they'll be glad that they won't have to blacken their hands."

Catherine, prompted by her father's last comment proudly held up her stained hands for her parents to see.

Somewhat ignoring Catherine, Francis said, "After you get through husking the walnuts, put them in the cabin so the squirrels won't get them."

Etta rolled her eyes. After all, she had taught Francis the necessity of doing so several years earlier after he unintentionally fed the squirrels following their displacement from Illinois and forced move to the Council Bluffs Reservation. "Wait!" she said as she stood up. "What's this about moving a cabin?"

"Oh!" responded Francis as he watched Catherine struggle to un-husk the remaining black walnuts. "Father Duerinck came out to the field the other day when I was breaking sod. He talked to me about wanting to live over by the Lasley's, but said there isn't any place for him to live there. Finally, he asked if he could borrow the one of ours that is empty. Of course, I would have to dismantle it and take it there. Bat can help me. Father Duerinck offered to pay me for moving the cabin."

Etta merely nodded her head to show that she understood what Francis said. However, her mind was not fixed on the unused cabin or the black walnuts but on being shot at and the shooting of Jack. She also felt that all of them should leave town. Her decision to leave Louisville was firmed up when Francis told her last night when they were looking at Jack about the death threats that he personally had received.

"What's happening?" asked Bat as he pulled up his

horse. Taking Matilda by the arm, Bat helped her dismount and slide to the ground. "By the way, where's Jack?" He was unaware that Jack had been shot and that his father had dragged Jack's carcass to a far off ravine with one of the oxen before any of the children woke up. He soon learned of the severity of the family's plight and his parents' decision to go to Michigan.

20 – Three Oaks

    Joseph Babeu looked up from his garden at the edge of Skunk Grove east of Joliet, Illinois, as he was clearing it of the dead plants from the summer's crops. He was astonished when he saw Etta being helped from the buggy that pulled up to the front of his cabin. "Watchekee!" exclaimed Joseph as he dropped his hoe, hopped over his split rail fence and warmly greeted Etta. Joseph's two boys who were helping him looked at each other somewhat stupefied. They had never seen their father so excited. "Archange!" Joseph shouted. "Come outside! Look who's here!" Archange poked her head out of the cabin and hesitated, but on seeing her old friend she broke into a run and gave Etta a big hug. Two more brown-faced children, the twin daughters of Joseph and Archange, bashfully watched from the safety of the cabin doorway.
    "Come inside," said Archange as she continued to hold Etta's hand. "You're just in time for supper. We're gonna have corn soup. Besides, it's too chilly out here. Come in by the fireplace and get warmed up before we eat."
    Archange noticed that Etta was unusually quiet during the meal and figured that she and Etta would have a nice visit after supper and the children were asleep. Archange put her children and those of Etta and Francis to bed early hoping to have a nice visit with Etta after eating. By the time Archange climbed down from the children's sleeping loft, Joseph and Francis were conversing by themselves. However, Etta already was fast asleep, curled up by the fireplace. Archange, though mildly disappointed, spread a blanket over Etta and thought, *"We can talk tomorrow. She's exhausted — travelling and taking care of her family."*

Archange woke up the next morning and saw that Francis had slept next to the fireplace. She expected that he would sleep next to Etta. However, Etta was gone. Archange started to get concerned when she heard the distinctive sound of someone vomiting. The sound came from the path that led from the cabin to outhouse. Quickly, Archange put on her coat and hurried outside. Seeing Watchekee bent over with a blanket draped over her shoulders and throwing up her morning breakfast, Archange, though shocked, suddenly realized why Watchekee was so exhausted after supper. She walked up to Watchekee, leaned over, and put her arm around her. Looking into her eyes Archange asked in a knowing way, "When?" Wiping her mouth, Watchekee said, "Next summer — about blackberry time."

During breakfast, Joseph and Francis soon found themselves discussing matters such as travel, weather and politics while Archange and Etta reminisced about their former experiences and their children. Towards the end of breakfast, the information that surfaced in the respective conversations was cross-shared with the respective spouses.

"Whadda you do here?" asked Francis.

"Me and Archange raise and sell vegetables. We sell most of our stuff to the Illinois and Michigan Canal workers in Joliet and Lockport. Until a few years ago, passengers on the canal also bought some of our vegetables. That was before the Chicago, Rock Island and Pacific Railroad was built. I also do some part-time jobs. By the way, are you and Watchekee — I can't get used to calling her Etta — planning to come back to Illinois?"

"No," replied Francis. "We're on our way to visit Etta's brother in Michigan. She hasn't seen him since about 1832. Besides things weren't too good in Kansas."

"How's that?"

"It was gettin' too dangerous for me and Etta. Etta got shot at, and I was gettin' death threats. A couple of weeks ago, my mule got shot."

"Why?"

"I was on the anti-slavery side. Someone didn't like us — especially me. When some guy shot my mule, me and Etta decided to leave for a while. In a couple of years, we'll go back. Don't have any land in Illinois, but we own ten lots in Louisville, Kansas. That's where we call home." As if talking to himself, Francis said "Gotta go back — some day." Then he realized that he was conversing with Joseph and turned to him, "Meanwhile, we'll travel around and visit old friends."

"Don't mean to pry, but how you gonna afford it."

"Etta keeps paying. She has a bag of gold. Keeps her gold in an ol' leather pouch. Don't know how she came by it. I've never pried much."

"Don't want any gold, but you can stay here. Stay the winter if you like and go up to Michigan next year."

****

"I liked what Joseph said," commented Etta as she and Francis were settling in for the second night. "It would be nice to stay here for awhile. All the children get along, but we need to get something for ourselves, especially if we stay the winter." "You're right," replied Francis as he started to fall asleep. Meanwhile, memories of the past, questions of how the present came about and what the future was going to be like for her unborn child kept churning through Etta's mind. The myriad of questions and concerns slightly tainted with fear prevented Etta from enjoying the rest that had overtaken Francis. By now, he was snoring so loudly that Etta could not fall asleep with or without the countless thoughts that flooded her mind.

The next morning Francis told Etta that he was going out to see if he could find work and a cabin that they could rent for a few months. Etta heard him when he returned late that night and shed his coat. She looked at Francis's face as he came in and sat down next to her, but could not read it. It was expressionless.

Archange sensing the awkwardness of the moment quickly said, "Francis, I will warm up something for you to eat."

Francis took his chair and pulled himself up to the rough-hewn table. Then with slight grin, he said, "Found work." "What? Where?" asked Etta excitedly as she wrapped her arms around Francis and gave him a hug. "Joseph gave me an idea when he mentioned the Illinois and Michigan Canal. So I rode over to a place called Lockport. I got a job on the canal. My experience working with mules helped me. The operators of the canal needed someone to drive mules along the tow path and pull barges." "Where's Lockport?" quizzically asked Etta. After swallowing a mouthful of bean soup, Francis nonchalantly said, "Not far."

Joseph wrinkled his brow and joined the conversation, "Lockport isn't far from here. But if you work on the canal, especially on the tow path, you'll be gone much of the time. Did you find a place to live?"

"No."

"When do you start?"

Wiping food from his mouth, Francis glanced at Etta and Joseph and said, "Three weeks. It'll give me time for Etta and me to find a place to live."

"Want to live here? I know that Watchekee — uh, Etta — and Archange like to visit," replied Joseph.

"We don't want to crowd you out."

"I don't mean in this cabin. We could build you your own cabin here in Skunk Grove. Etta and Archange already have talked about the idea."

While reaching for a piece of corn bread, Francis threw a glance at Etta who nodded her head in agreement to what Joseph just said. Recognizing that an agreement already had been reached, Francis asked, "How you and me gonna put up a cabin in three weeks?"

Joseph had a ready answer. "Margarite Naschah and her husband, Leon Bourassa, live on the south side of Skunk Grove. I can get Leon to help. Actually, there are a few other Potawatomi families in the area. Think we can get other men to help. Etta, remember Naschah and Leon from Council Bluffs?"

"I sure do," answered Etta with a broad smile. "Didn't know they left."

"A few came back about the same time we did. We have the start of a small Potawatomi village here," chuckled Joseph.

Skunk Grove was a reservation given to Archange per the 1832 Treaty of Camp Tippecanoe. The presence of other Potawatomi who lived in Skunk Grove made Etta feel comfortable. The comfort was main reason why Etta and Francis decided to stay in the area over the coming winter.

Winter extended to spring, and it wasn't until the following June that they left to visit Etta's brother in Michigan. By this time, Joseph had come to greatly appreciate Bat's help in the vegetable garden. Because of this and the kinship that Matilda and Catherine had with the Babeu's children, it was decided the all three would stay with the Babeu's until Etta and Francis returned.

"Sure you don't want to stay here until you have your baby? Remember, I helped deliver your baby at Princeton. That was nearly twenty years ago! You named her after me so I must have been a pretty good mid-wife," chatted Archange knowing that Etta was intent on leaving soon for Michigan even though she was far into her pregnancy

Little did Etta know that the peace she and her family felt in Skunk Grove was a political and cultural paradox. Archange's reservation in the grove of majestic oaks land was traceable to one of the same treaty that ultimately brought undue hardships and sadness to the mid-wife who was to deliver Etta's next baby.

****

    Archange spotted Etta and Francis as they were approaching her cabin in their buggy. She clearly saw that Etta was holding a cradle board in her lap. Dropping her wooden water bucket, she hollered, "Bat, Matilda, Catherine, your mother and father are back! Come out here! They have a baby with them! I don't know if you have a new sister or brother! Hurry! Let's find out! Joseph! Where are you? Etta and Francis are back!"

    Archange and Joseph soon found out that Etta and Francis barely had gotten into Michigan when Etta's labor pains started. "We had to stop in, I think in a village called Three Oaks. Etta had Charles there," crowed Francis. "That was only about six weeks ago."

    "Did you have to deliver Charles yourself?" inquired Archange.

    "I thought I was gonna have to," answered Francis who first looked at Charles and then smilingly at Etta.

    "Who helped you then?" asked Archange.

    "It turned out that we had just met a lady who said her name was Ko-bun-da. When she saw Etta's condition she offered to help us. Said that she had one of her babies in the woods by herself and didn't want us to go through what she did."

    "Why did she a baby in such horrible conditions?"

    "According to her, her people in northern Indiana were forced to go to eastern Kansas," answered Francis. "She blamed some of the problems on a treaty made at the Tippecanoe River in 1832. She called it a 'whiskey treaty.'"

    "Yes," interjected Etta. "Her husband, Sinegaw, was made to go too. He had gone to a meeting at a chapel at

Menominee's village. It was supposed to have been a friendly meeting. It wasn't. Kbunda was warned and escaped to the woods at the same time her baby came. At first, neither of them knew if the other was dead or alive. Sinegaw eventually made it back and found her. According to Kbunda, he was very weak from his struggle to get back and find her. He became an alcoholic and died — must have been on many 'high lonesomes.' I know some of the Potawatomi who were forced to go on the long march. Some of them lost their grandparents and small children."

Joseph who had been chopping down trees to expand his garden, shook wood chips off his bare chest and asked, "Gonna stay here? At least through the coming winter again?"

"Yes, we'd like to stay awhile, but Etta is anxious to see Will up in Galena. Probably head out in the spring, about the time when dogwoods start blooming."

"I got so excited about seeing your baby that I forgot to ask you about your brother. Did you see him?" asked Archange looking at Etta and holding her baby.

"Yes, we saw him," said Etta. "We found him in Pokagon's village along the Saint Joseph River. However, Pam-dosh didn't seem very excited to see us. He glared at Francis when they met. Made us feel sort of uncomfortable. His wife made a special meal for us, bear paw stew. Still we didn't feel welcome, so we stayed only one night and left the next morning. Sleeping in a wigwam brought back many memories of the time I was a little girl growing up along the Pickamick."

"Pickamick? People around here now call it the Iroquois River. Oh well, I'm glad you're back. Come in and rest. You and Francis can settle into your cabin later today," said Archange running her fingers through the black, fuzzy hair of Charles. "Have you baptized him yet?"

"No" replied Etta. "After we get rested, we'll take him to St. Patrick's Church in Joliet. That's where Bat was baptized. We want Father DuPontavice to baptize him. Like he did Bat."

"Father DuPontavice isn't there anymore. He went to someplace in Indiana. Father Maurice de Saint Palais is serving at St. Patrick's now."

"I was hoping to see Father DuPontavice, but we'll go to St. Patrick's anyway. Don't think we should wait until we get back to Kansas."

****

Bat already was holding the reins of the buggy horses when Etta plopped Charles on the seat next to him and climbed aboard herself. He brotherly pulled Charles next to him and put one arm around him to keep him from falling to the floor board, but Charles still squirmed, trying to escape the restraint. Bat held him tightly because the buggy was full of luggage and camping provisions. Furthermore, Francis, Matilda and Catherine were yet to find sitting places in the loaded buggy. Time had come for the Bergeron family to leave the comforts of Skunk Grove.

Francis and Joseph came out of Joseph's cabin together exchanging good-byes and Joseph telling Francis the best way to get to Galena. The younger children, both the Bergeron's and the Babeu's were playing, oblivious to the thought that they probably would never see each other again.

Archange was standing next to Etta who, after she got seated, started helping her daughters, Matilda and Catherine, get into the back seat of the buggy. Finally, Francis climbed in shoving Bat into the middle of the driver's seat so that he was between him and his mother. Still, Bat held onto the reins. Finally, Francis looked at Bat and nodded. Seeing the indication that all was ready, Bat shouted "Giddy up!" and smartly snapped the reins.

21 – The Tannery

Etta and Francis were advised that finding William Chobart in Galena might be difficult because the town was bustling with activity relating to the lead mines in the area. All Etta knew regarding his whereabouts is what Mesawkequa told her during their last visit in St. Mary's. Namely, he ran a tannery in Galena. Etta and Francis were flabbergasted when they saw just how busy the town was when they arrived. Seeing that the activity seemed to center around the loading docks next to the Galena River, they used the area to see if anybody knew him.

Loud horn blasts signaled the dock workers in Galena that the S.S. Carrie V. Kountz was off the Mississippi and heading up the Galena River. What already was a high level of activity soon became a blur of human bodies. It was as if an ant hill had been kicked. Workers scurried around where the river boat soon would be docking to unload its cargo and passengers. Some of the workers had empty carts and wagons. Others were readying gang planks or sitting on materials needing to be loaded onto the approaching paddle-wheeler.

Etta instructed her older children to stay in the buggy, but picked up Charles as she and Francis began strolling around the dock area inquiring about a William Chobart. Etta, as she squeezed the upper arm of Francis with her free hand asked in a somewhat panic-stricken voice, "Will we ever find him?"

Their wandering gave them an opportunity to look at the town and the surrounding hills. Never before had Etta seen so much activity. Plumes of smoke arose from the chimneys of smelters that were extracting lead from the ore mined in the surrounding hills. Reflectant bars of lead that were to be loaded on the approaching river boat filled many of the carts.

Looking at the hills north and south of Galena, Etta commented to Francis, "The hills don't have any trees on them." She later learned that most of the trees had been cut to provide fuel for the many smelters in the town.

"Excuse me," Francis said somewhat timidly to a passing worker. The worker was pushing a heavy cargo cart and acted as if he didn't hear him.

Looking around, Etta was surprised to see an Indian man standing by a cart piled with tanned furs and giving orders to a white man. She walked over to the man who had caught her attention and while shifting Charles to another hip said, "Pardon me. I'm Mrs. Bergeron. My husband and me just got here. We're lookin' for a William Chobart. He runs a tannery and was wonderin' if you know him 'cause you've got some pelts."

"Know him? I work for him!" replied the man. "By the way, I'm Ely Parker." He readily noticed that Etta was staring at him and said, "Yes, I'm Indian — Seneca. And you?"

"Potawatomi," answered Etta.

Ely chuckled, "We used to raid you!"

Etta unhesitatingly countered, "I know — until we defeated you in Illinois near my village. My grandparents told me about the fight."

Realizing that Etta was not to be outdone, Ely quickly said, "As soon as I get this load of furs on board, I'll take you to Mr. Chobart."

Francis came over to where Etta and Ely were talking. Growing concerned about the children and upon learning that Ely could take Etta to the man they were looking for, he excused himself by saying, "Etta, I need to go back to the children. They're probably getting restless by now. Where can I find you later?"

Francis started leaving to go back to his three children when Etta asked, "Francis, can you take Charles? I fed him just before we got into town." Then in a hushed voice she added, "If he does get fussy, give him a sugar teat."

"Oh!" said Ely as Francis was taking Charles from Etta. "We're going directly to Mr. Chobart's tannery or his house across the street from it. The tannery is about six blocks this way." Ely pursed his lips and slightly moved his head to the left, indicating the direction that Francis needed to go. "The odor of the tannery will let you know when you are getting close!" he laughed.

Etta soon found herself following Ely through the winding streets of Galena. Pausing in front of a shop along the river after walking several blocks from the loading dock area, he said, "This is William's tannery." Pointing with his lips, he continued, "He lives across the street in that little house on the corner. His son, George William — likes to be called Will — lives with him. If William isn't in the tannery, he most likely is with Will. Will is very sick."

Walking into the dimly lighted tannery, Etta spotted a familiar figure, short but stout. Ely walked over to his boss who was busy scraping a fresh hide and said in his ear, "William, this woman wants to see you." William gruffly said, "I'm busy!" However, he managed to take a quick look at his visitor. Instantly, he whirled around and exclaimed, "Watchekee!" Ely was smiling but dumbfounded. He wisely thought it best to find work while William and Mrs. Bergeron animatedly talked.

After the initial euphoria of seeing Etta, William hung his head and said, "Will is sick. The doctor said that he has TB."

"Yes, I know. Mesawkequa told me," said Etta as she put her hand on William's shoulder.

Lifting his head, William replied "Mesawkequa? Heard she's in Kansas. You there too? Noel told me that you got married to a Francis Bergeron. Guess to be proper, I should call you Mrs. Bergeron — thought you were in Council Bluffs."

"Yes, I'm Mrs. Bergeron but most people call me Etta now. Like Mesawkequa, we live in Kansas too — Louisville, Kansas."

"Whatcha doing here?"

"I've come to take care of Will. Want to make him well."

"Don't know if anyone can help him. He's in bed across the street. If you want, I'll take you to see him."

Tears rolled down Will's cheeks when he saw Etta standing in the doorway of his bedroom. Light from his bedroom window illuminated a familiar face he thought he would never see again. To Will, Etta was his mother. After all, she took care of him after Mesawkequa left. Etta too had tears in her eyes as did Will's father. Before them lay Will, now a young man of six feet but one so stricken that he was close to death.

"Mother," he tried to say, but his coughing and blood cut off the rest of his sentence.

Etta cradled Will in her arms for a few minutes. It was a poignant, heart wrenching reunion as a beam of sunlight cascaded down on them, one so healthy, one so sick. Then she quietly left the bedroom when Will seemingly fell asleep.

Going outside and sitting in the warmth of the late spring sun, Etta found herself unsure of what to do. As she pondered the situation, she heard the clip-clop of horse hooves. Looking up, she saw the familiar faces of her family coming down the street. When the buggy stopped in front of William's house, Etta stood up and slowly walked to the street. The look on Etta's face told Francis that she was greatly troubled. "Whoa!" Francis commanded as he tugged on the reins and brought his team of horses to a halt. He jumped out of the buggy and embraced Etta who began to cry as she buried her face against his chest.

Ely had remained outside the tannery when Etta and William went to see Will. Viewing the scene that had just unfolded, he strolled across the street to see if he could help in any way. First he looked at William, then at Francis and the buggy filled with children. Even though he did not fully know what was happening or how Mrs. Bergeron happened to know his boss, he offered, "Mr. and Mrs. Bergeron, you and your children are welcome to spend the night at my place. I will tell my wife, Sarah, that you are coming." Pointing the direction with his lips, he added, "We live two blocks that way. It is the only house on the block on this side of the street. Mr. Bergeron, there is room in the little barn behind the house for your horses. You will find hay and oats for them too. Help yourself."

Francis nodded his head in appreciation as he shook Ely's hand.

22 – Bag of Gold

Etta left Will's bedroom. She was too exhausted to cry. Finding a pair of scissors in the living room, she cut off the single, thick braid of hair that cascaded down her back. It was her Potawatomi way of saying that she was in mourning. Only twice before had she cut her hair. The first time was nearly 30 years earlier when her infant daughter by Hubbard died in Danville, Illinois. The second time was when Madeline died after being bitten by the copper head. The death of Will was expected, yet it was an emotional year in which Etta was almost constantly at Will's bed side hoping that Will would somehow recover.

Nearly a year had gone by since Etta and Francis had decided that she should stay to care for Will. Mutually agreed to, Francis returned to Kansas and waited for Etta to come home. Olivie helped take care of Matilda and Catherine once he got back to Louisville, Kansas. Bat, who was now a strapping teenager, worked in the wheat and hay fields while Francis got his job back at Louis Vieux's toll bridge. The question of what to do with Charles had been solved when Sarah graciously offered to babysit him whenever Etta was caring for Will.

****

One week after Will's burial, Etta and William walked from his house to the Butterfield Stage Coach House close to the river in downtown Galena. William was very quiet as they walked along. His head drooped. The only thing that seemed to be cheery was the sunshine. The last two days of torrential rains had delayed Etta's departure. One block from the coach house, William finally said in a subdued voice, "Thanks for coming. I know that it meant a lot to Will."

"I wish that I could have done more to help him," replied Etta stepping around a rain puddle and steering the teetering Charles away from it.

"You made him comfortable."

Neither of them spoke for the next two blocks. The only sounds were of their footsteps and an occasional sniffle by Etta who unsuccessfully was trying to hold back tears.

William, familiar with the neighborhood, looked up. Ahead of him he saw that the stage coach already had arrived and was loading passengers and baggage for the return trip to Peoria. "Guess we had better hurry!" he said. "Need some fare money?"

"No," said Etta as she reached into her purse and pulled out a leather pouch.

William did a double take and came out of his solemn trance when he saw the bag Etta was holding. It bore a white-beaded letter N. "Isn't that the bag that Noel used to keep his gold in?" asked William.

"It used to be. He gave it to me!" she said with a degree uncharacteristic smugness.

A slight smile came across William's face. What he heard seemingly brought him out of the darkness that had overcome him when he first learned that Will had TB. "Noel told me about the time when he saw you when you came back. He said he took you down to his store to tell you to get lost. He got so flustered that he threw a bag of money at you." Laughing, William continued his recollection of what Noel said, "He thought he was throwing a bag of silver at you, not his gold! Serves him right!"

"Get in, madam, if you're going!" shouted the coach driver to Etta.

William threw Etta's clothes bag to the top of the stage

coach and helped Etta and Charles get aboard. As the coach began to pull away, he yelled, "Transfer to Kankakee when you get to Peoria! Greet Marianne! Noel told me that he sent her to a mission school in Florissant, Missouri, and that she had come back — that was about ten years ago!

Etta was anxious to go back to Kansas, but Mesawkequaw asked her to see Marianne when she was in Illinois. *"Too bad me and Francis didn't go to Bourbonnais Grove when we were in Skunk Grove,"* she thought.

The Butterfield Stage Coach jostled Etta and the other passengers as they rolled up and down the steep hills of northwestern Illinois. The ride was exceptionally rough because the heavy rains had left the wagon roads muddy and full of deep ruts. Etta tried to block out the pain from being constantly thrown against the side of the coach's interior by thinking of the people she anticipated seeing and what might lie ahead, *"Marianne, the Vail's — Noel — If I happen to see him, I'll try to be cordial. — William said Kankakee. He must have meant Bourbonnais Grove."*

23 – Homecoming

Etta recognized him and the store. He was stooped and had a shock of white hair, but it was him. "Stop!" she shouted to the driver of the fast moving stage coach.

Almost unaware of the driver's command to the team to stop, Etta jumped out of the stage coach and quickly retrieved her baggage after it was thrown and landed on the dusty road. Hurrying back to the store that nearly had been passed, Etta saw a man's figure going inside. "Mr. Rantz! Mr. Rantz!" she yelled. The man stopped. Squinting, he scarcely could see that a woman was waving her arms at him. He stood in the doorway as Etta, grinning broadly, walked toward him. Suddenly, he recognized her.

Sitting under the same tree where Francis talked to Archange and Joseph several years earlier, Etta started telling Mr. Rantz about what she and Francis were doing, what had happened to them, and where they were living now. Smoke drifted up from the bowl of his clay pipe as Rantz listened intently to Etta. He leaned forward to hear her because of a hearing loss attributable to age. Rantz also had the unfortunate experience of having a rowdy customer accidentally shoot a muzzle loader close to his left ear while outside the store examining a deer that the customer had shot in the nearby woods.

Rantz's pipe went out while Etta talked. As he always did on such occasions, Rantz unsheathed his knife and loosened the pipe's ashes with it. While carefully rapping the pipe against the heel of his boot, he asked, "What brings you out this way?"

Etta was excited about seeing Rantz. Quickly, her

disposition changed. Looking up and taking a deep breath, she said, "I came to take care of Will. Remember him? Mesawkequa's and William Chobart's son."

"Yes, I remember him. Used to see him sometimes — a couple of years ago at Noel's. Then he left. Heard he went to live with his father in Galena. By chance have you been up there?"

"Yes. Will got real sick. He got TB."

"He must be better if you're down here now."

"No," answered Etta as she lowered her head and turned from Rantz to hide her tears.

Rantz then noticed that Etta had recently cut her braid and asked, "Are you telling me he died?"

"Yes, about ten days ago," replied Etta in a hushed voice.

Rantz leaned back on his stool and took a deep breath of his own. "We've had some sadness here too. Marianne also died — about nine or ten years ago. Seems that she picked up something down at the school where Noel sent her. Was your sister her mother? I know that Noel was her father."

Etta nearly was unable to comprehend what Rantz had just told her as a new wave of remorse swept over her. After several moments of silence while looking straight ahead, she sadly said, "Marianne was one of the reasons why I came here before returning to Kansas."

****

Noel's brick house was an impressive sight in Bourbonnais Grove. Etta and Charles stood in its front yard as buggies rolled behind them. The drivers were unaware of the emotions and memories that were flooding Etta's mind. Slowly, she walked up to the front door and knocked. The moment was much different then when she had barged into the house upon returning from Council Bluffs eighteen years earlier. At the time, she confronted the new Mrs. LeVasseur. This time, Etta was reticent and only wanted to express her condolences.

The front door slowly opened. Etta and Noel stood facing each other. Noel was expressionless when he saw Etta. Finally, he politely held the door open farther and said, "Please — come in."

Sitting in the parlor were Mrs. LeVasseur and to Etta's surprise, Phoebe, Sid Vail's sister. At first, Noel's wife seemed threatened by Etta's presence; but when Phoebe warmly and enthusiastically greeted her, she relaxed. Etta, sensing that she was mildly welcome, graciously accepted Mrs. LeVasseur's invitation to sit and join them.

****

Etta's mind continued to race with memories, some pleasant, others unpleasant, while returning to Kansas after her sojourn to Bourbonnais Grove from Galena. Her sadness regarding the deaths of Will and Marianne were erased by the joy that she would soon be home seeing Francis and their children. As the stage coach carrying her approached Louis Vieux's toll bridge, she excitedly anticipated that she would surprise Francis and that he would take her up in his arms. She was the one who was surprised.

As anticipated, Louis happily welcomed her back as she stepped off the stage coach at the bridge while the driver paid Louis. However, she looked around and did not see Francis. Worried, she asked Louis, "Where's Francis?"

"He quit three weeks ago! He said he needed time to get a place ready for you because he figured that you would be back sometime late this summer."

"Wait!" shouted Etta to the driver of the stage coach. It had started to cross the bridge without her. Tugging at Charles, she hurriedly climbed aboard, clutching her clothes bag in her lap. "*How'm I gonna find him?*" she thought.

Etta climbed out of the coach when it stopped at Louisville's stage coach station and was welcomed home by Hank, the station manager. Etta and Francis both knew Hank, but she was more worried about finding Francis than talking to Hank. Etta remembered that Francis said she would have a real house when she got back, but didn't say where. When Hank finished dealing with the three other passengers who had arrived, Etta asked, "Hank, do you know where I can find Francis?"

Hank customarily grinned as he talked. Unfortunately, his smile now revealed that his two upper front teeth were missing. They and three other teeth were knocked out when Hank took on a roving boxer in the nearby village square. Hank received a vicious right upper cut and was knocked out in the first twenty seconds of the fight. Everybody whooped and hollered until they saw blood squirting out of Hank's nose and mouth. "Yep!" he answered. "Francis figured that you would be home the first part of fall. You're here early though I didn't really know when you'd be back! Francis arranged for Henry Heinecke to take you to the new place whenever you got back if he weren't in town himself. Francis said you'd have a youngster with you. You sure do! Wait here. I'll get Henry for you. I saw him go into my livery a couple of minutes ago."

Etta looked down the street as she waited and saw the cabin that used to be her home.

Turning the other direction, she saw Hank and Henry approaching. "Afternoon, Mrs. Bergeron," said Henry tipping his hat. "Francis asked me to take you to your new place should it be necessary. I haven't seen him today, but I'll be glad to hitch up my horse and give you a ride. Ready? Say, who's with you?"

"This is Charles. He was two last month."

Patting Charles on the head, Henry said, "Stay right

here. I'll be back in a few minutes."

Riding to the north side of Louisville, Etta noticed that the fall flowers were starting to bloom. Henry saw her looking at them. He always enjoyed talking to her about plants and the traditional uses of them. Because goldenrods and sunflowers were really prolific, Henry anticipated that he could get some information as he drove Etta to her new house. "Did any of your people ever use goldenrods for anything?" he asked.

"The flowers make a good yellow dye. Medicine was made from its roots," she answered. Etta then went strangely quiet as she got lost in her thoughts about Will, *"The medicine that I made for him didn't do any good. It should've helped him get over his bad cough."*

"Excuse me, Mrs. Bergeron. Your house is around the curve. I think that you will like the place where Francis and the children are living."

Etta gasped when she saw her new house, but what really caught her attention was seeing Matilda and Catherine playing with dolls in the front yard under the shade of a chinquapin oak. *"They remind me so much of Olivie and Archange when they were young, and we were living on the bluff above the Missouri River,"* she thought. As the buggy descended the last hill and started to make its way into the lane leading up to the house, Etta's shaggy black and white dog began barking.

"Quiet! It's just one of them squirrels!" yelled Matilda. She and Catherine remained focused on the dolls. Meanwhile, Bat, riding bareback, had just come in the field on his horse and was curious as to what the dog was barking. As he rode around the house, he saw the buggy and wondered who had come to visit. "Mother! It's mother! Mother's home!" he yelled excitedly.

Matilda and Catherine jerked up their heads and looked at the buggy that had just entered the yard. Seeing their long absent mother and brother, they dropped their dolls, squealed in delight, and ran to Etta and Charles who by now were getting out of the buggy. Reaching their mother, they began tugging at her skirt and looking up at her to make certain they could get their share of attention. They essentially were strangers to Charles who stood wide-eyed as he clutched his mother's leg for security.

Seeing that his presence no longer was needed, Henry unloaded and dropped Etta's bag to the ground and left after Etta thanked him. He started humming as he drove up the hill that overlooked the Bergeron farmstead. When he turned the curve and headed back into Louisville, he stopped his tune and thought to himself, *"I wonder who will be the happiest to see Mrs. Bergeron come back, Francis or the children?"* He then put his horse into a fast trot.

Bat already was galloping back to the prairie where his father was cutting the last crop of hay. Hearing Bat shouting "Mother's home!" Francis dropped his scythe in disbelief as Bat pulled up his horse beside him. Wiping the perspiration from his forehead, Francis leaped onto the horse behind his son. Riding double, Bat and his father headed for the house.

It was later than usual before the older children could be convinced to go to bed. Matilda and Catherine finally went to their small bedroom behind the living room. Charles already was asleep in his little bed in the corner of the girls' bedroom. Just as Bat went upstairs to his bedroom in the attic, Matilda stuck out her head and asked concernedly, "Mother, will you be here in the morning?"

Etta began blowing out the oil lamps that gave the living room a warm glow. When she got to the last lamp, she paused and looked longingly at Francis. "Where's our bedroom?" she asked seductively as she extinguished the flickering flame of the last lamp.

24 – Horde of Grasshoppers

"Had any problems since you got back from Illinois?" asked Etta.

"No," responded Francis, eating his fried eggs.

"How about Jack? Ever find out who shot him?"

"Not really. But I think I know who — the former sheriff of LeCompton, Sam Jones, or at least a crony of his."

"Why do you think he might've done it?"

"Just a hunch. Jones got mad when Kansas voted to be a free state. He burned down the hotel in Lawrence about the time Charles was born. Lawrence is active in the anti-slavery movement. He burned down the hotel there to get even."

After several minutes, Etta started laughing.

Francis put down his coffee cup and said, "I don't think the hotel gettin' burned is funny."

"No! No!" giggled Etta. "Hank's missin' his front teeth!"

"Oh! That! A travelin' boxer knocked them out. I saw it happen shortly after I got back," smiled Francis, but was thinking about what happened to Jack and how grateful he was for not having received any death threats since returning because of his anti-slavery position.

Before Etta and Francis could talk any more, Matilda came into the small kitchen area rubbing her eyes and wanting breakfast. Francis looked at Etta and then spoke to Matilda, "Run out to the chicken shed and find some eggs. Get enough for your sister and brothers too."

Matilda obediently scooted out the door and headed for the chicken coop. In a few minutes she came back carrying seven eggs in a towel. "Phew!" she said as she came through the front door. "Mko found a skunk last night! He really got it!"

After all the children were roused and fed, Etta asked them to go play outside. Bat understood that his mother and father wanted to talk so he excused himself, "Got some work to do."

"How'd you get this place and why here?" asked Etta with a quizzical look on her face.

"Why? Let's go for a ride and I will explain. How? I'll answer how after I answer your why."

Francis went to the tack room and began harnessing the buggy horse. As he was hitching up his the buggy, Etta yelled to the children, "Matilda, watch the others until your father and me get back!"

Francis drove down a little used wagon path that went across a prairie where they came across Bat who was raking the hay that his father had scythed the day before. "You've cut a lot of hay. It's more than you ever cut for Anthony Tescier. What you gonna do with all of it?" commented Etta. Francis didn't answer because he was focused on fording Rock Creek. After getting across the creek, he turned left onto a well-worn wagon road. Etta looked at the road and said, "This is the Oregon Trail. Louis's bridge can't be too far behind us."

"Yep!" replied Francis as he put the horse into a faster trot. "Wait until you see what is just ahead of us." As they rounded a curve in the Oregon Trail a wide expanse was revealed. Off to one side was a large spring gushing out of a limestone bluff. Its water flowed into Rock Creek. "This is Scott Spring!" said Francis as if to impress Etta.

"So? What's so great about it?"

"Where is Louis's bridge?" Francis asked. Without giving Etta time to respond, he continued, "On the Oregon Trail, right? It's made him rich, right? The same immigrants who cross the bridge stop here overnight. There's plenty of water, but they need forage for their oxen teams and horses plus any cattle they have with them. You saw the hay that Bat's raking. We'll bring it here next year and sell it. I plan to break some sod this fall and plant a field of corn next year. In two years, we'll sell it too."

"You've pretty much answered my why. Now tell me how."

"The Eggers's used to live on the farm. Mr. Eggers told me that he's too old to work hard any more. He knew that we own ten lots in Louisville and asked if I wanted to trade properties. After I realized where his farm was at, I began thinking about how I could sell forage and feed to the immigrants. The only problem is that you were gone. I thought you would agree with me when you got back so Mr. Eggers said let's trade now and finalize the switch when you got back."

Francis began growing concerned that Etta was not favorable to the 'how' because Etta didn't say anything about what he said at Scott Spring or during most of the trip home. She finally looked up at Francis, locked her arm in his and said, "Good trade!" as she laid her head against his shoulder.

The 'good trade' became disastrous starting with the second summer and continuing until the early 1860's. First, a severe drought hit. Whereas the extreme dryness prevented much of the corn to grow and mature, the prairie grasses were not affected. The result was not having field corn to sell to the immigrants at Scott Spring even though there was hay — for the present time. However, the lack of rain didn't prevent a horde of grasshoppers from nearly devastating even the prairie grasses. The unpredictability of rain and destruction by the grasshoppers put an end to Francis's dream of selling corn and hay to the immigrants on the Oregon Trail.

25 – Lieutenant Murphy's Message

"Where's Bat? Have you seen him? The cow's been milked, but his horse is gone." Etta worriedly said in a raised voice to Francis while she cracked the eggs that Matilda and Catherine had gathered. Francis nonchalantly hollered into the kitchen while pulling on his boots, "Probably left early to cut some hay. Probably wants to beat the heat. It's gonna be hot today! By the looks of the sky, we won't get any rain today. I expect that he'll be back by noon."

Bat never came home. Several weeks went by. His disappearance was beginning to affect Etta and the rest of the family. She remembered, "*My brother disappeared when I was living in the Pickamick River village. My mother, Monashki, may have grieved, but nothing was said. Wasn't until years later that I learned he had gone to live in Michigan.*" Finally, Etta broke down and fell into Francis's arms.

Two days later, Francis said, "Etta, I need to go into Louisville and get a salt block. I should be back around supper time." As he drove his buggy down the lane leading from the house, he turned and waved to Etta and the children who had gathered by the front door. "*The house needs a front porch,*" he thought. Once he got to Louisville, Francis bought his salt block at the feed store, adjacent to Hank's Livery. Hank was standing in front of the stage coach house when he saw Francis go into the feed store and ran across the street to talk to him.

"Mornin', Francis."

"Hello, Hank. Mornin' to you too."

"Glad to see you Francis. I's hopin' to see you one of these days. I've got somethin' you'll be interested in. It's somethin' 'bout Bat."

"WHAT'S THAT?" asked Francis carrying the salt block to his buggy and heaving it onto the buggy's floor.

"Jake come in on the stage from Ft. Riley yesterday mornin'. He'd gone there to have his contract for flour signed by the post's adjutant. Anyway, while he was waitin' he seen Bat."

Francis who usually tried to avoid Hank because of his verbosity said attentively, "Go on!"

"Well," continued Hank, "Jake seen Bat like I said. He's a ridin' along with a column of troops goin' out patrolin' like he's a scout. Another scout was with him accordin' to Jake."

Hank was still talking when Francis leaped into his buggy and grabbed the reins. "Thanks for the information. Hank, you gave me some good news. I know that Etta will be much relieved to hear it." "Gidda up, Belle!"

Francis was planning to stop by the courthouse and see Henry Heinecke, but changed his mind and drove home as fast as he could get Belle to trot.

"Whoa, Belle!" shouted Francis, commanding her to stop when he got to his farm.

Etta and the children were in the side yard when Francis came driving up to the house. Most of them were taking turns scrubbing clothes in the shade. As soon as a pile of clothes got washed, Matilda and Catherine took them to a nearby split rail fence to dry in the sun. Charles, meanwhile, was pulling on the cat's ears. The cat, switching her tail, seemed to enjoy the attention she was getting but also seemed annoyed.

Francis quickly tied Belle to a hackberry tree and walked over to Etta and put his arms around her. She saw how Francis had raced Belle down the lane and didn't know what was happening until Francis happily said, "Bat's at Fort Riley! He's a scout!" Hearing this, Etta's inner turmoil quickly vanished, and she squealed with glee. After Etta and Francis mutually hugged, she turned, crossed herself and clasped her hands in a thankful prayer.

****

Sumac and sassafras leaves were turning red, a harbinger of the coming season. Etta got up early to start a fire in the black, pot belly stove in the small kitchen so that she could make coffee. Its aroma lured Francis out of the bedroom. Sliding a chair next to the stove, he sat down and graciously took the cup of coffee that Etta handed to him. After a few slurps, he spoke. "Yesterday when I was cutting firewood, I saw lots of wild grapes. Are you interested in getting some to make jelly? Suppose I hitch up the buckboard so we all can go? We can pretty much fill the back of the wagon with all that I saw down by the creek. Matilda and Catherine might have to climb up in the trees to pick some of them."

Etta asked, "I thought you needed to get hay?"

"We already got enough to see us through the coming winter," answered Francis.

Charles came into the kitchen before his mother could respond. He soon was followed by Matilda and Catherine. Etta nodded "yes" and turned to dish up some hot oatmeal for her hungry family.

****

Lieutenant Sean Murphy rode up to the Bergeron farm house late in the afternoon. It had been a long ride for him. After dismounting from his horse, he strolled up to the front door and knocked. There was no answer. *"There's not even a dog to greet me,"* he thought and slapped the envelope he was holding, *"but I have orders to hand this message to the*

Bergeron's." As he stood by the door holding the envelope and pondering what to do, he heard the distinctive sound of rolling wagon wheels and the clip-clop of horse hooves as they struck the ground. Lieutenant Murphy then looked around the corner of the house and saw what he assumed was the Bergeron family.

The family looked quite happy. Etta and Francis were in the driver's seat with Matilda between them. She was holding the reins and driving the team of two draft horses. Catherine was sitting on the floorboard just behind her parents. Her arms were loosely wrapped around Charles so that she could catch her brother should he have the notion to jump out of the wagon. Together, they looked as if they were guarding the wild grapes piled high behind them.

Francis, seeing that they had company, told Matilda to drive to the front of the house. When their dog sensed Lieutenant Murphy's horse, he quickly ran ahead to assume his protective duties. The nature his of barks and growls indicated that he was confronting a stranger.

Upon seeing the army officer, Francis took the reins from Matilda, commanded his team to stop and pulled the wagon's brake handle. "Matilda, take your sister and brother into the house," he said as he and Etta worriedly looked at each other.

"Good afternoon, madam and you too, sir. Are you Mr. and Mrs. Bergeron?"

"Yes," said Francis hesitantly. He could feel Etta gripping his arm.

"I'm Lieutenant Murphy from Fort Riley. I have a message for you about your son."

26 – The Post Surgeon

Francis read and re-read the message that Lieutenant Murphy had delivered the day before as he and Etta hurried their horse-drawn buggy down the Military Road leading to Fort Riley:

"I regret to inform you that your son, John Baptiste, was gravely wounded one week ago in the performance of his duties. While scouting for his unit, which was on routine patrol, he was ambushed by a renegade party of Pawnee warriors. Thanks to the quick action of bravery by his fellow scout, Mr. Wesley Lewis, he was saved from certain death. Presently, your son is hospitalized at Fort Riley. I am unable to tell you how long his recovery will be. He requested that you be notified.

Sincerely,

Colonel Ervin Pugsley II, M.D.
Post Surgeon
Fort Riley"

****

"Please hurry!" said Etta in a concerned voice.
"Belle is exhausted! I can't get her to go any faster, but we should get there soon! Hope that she can make it the rest of the way!" replied Francis.
Etta and Francis skirted along the Kansas River for 38

miles from Louisville. After stopping in Manhattan for one night, Fort Riley finally came into view. Its buildings were constructed from the area's abundant limestone. Subsequently, the complex of the fort's buildings looked like an assemblage of huge yellowish boulders except linear orderliness prevailed.

"What's the fort for?" asked Etta as they approached.

"Supposedly to protect the white settlers on the Oregon and Santa Fe trails."

"Protect them from what?"

"You!"

At the entry gate to Fort Riley, Francis brought his buggy to a quick halt. Belle clearly was winded and didn't even rear in response to having the bit jerked in her mouth. Belle was soaked in perspiration, and foam dripped from her mouth as she mouthed the bit in a futile effort to spit it out. After getting permission to enter and getting directions to the hospital ward, Francis snapped the buggy whip on the Belle's back. It was no use. Belle snorted and pawed the road with one fore-hoof, refusing to go any farther.

"Just like Jack!" muttered Francis. Unceremoniously, he pulled Etta from the buggy, and the two of them hurried in the direction of the hospital ward to see Bat.

"What about Belle?" asked Etta as she held onto her bonnet.

Francis seemingly ignored her. *"Someone will move Belle — some time. I'll find her later!"* he thought to himself as he and Etta briskly walked along to find the fort's hospital.

Unsure of where they were at, Francis asked a passing red-haired man dressed in a gray shirt and fringed buckskin pants, "Can you please tell us how to get to the hospital building?"

The man pointed behind him while walking down a few steps from the front porch of the yellow, limestone buildings and said, "You're here. Go through that door."

"Thanks!" said Francis. *"He doesn't look like a dragoon. No kind of uniform."*

Taking a deep breath and recovering from his hurried steps, Francis, unlike his disposition just a few minutes earlier, gently took Etta's arm and motioned for her to go into the hospital. They went in not knowing what to expect.

Never before had Etta seen such a building. The wooden door opening into it was large and heavy. It creaked as it was opened and closed. Immediately inside the front door was a foyer. Its floor had been constructed of the same stones as the building's walls.

Sitting in a straight-back chair at a desk in the entryway was a dragoon, with the rank of sergeant, going through a pile of papers that were the patients' medical charts. Other than the medical charts, the only other items on the desk were an oil lamp, a crow quill pen and a bottle of ink. In a quiet, methodical manner, the dragoon was working through the charts. It was obvious that he had been working through the charts because one stack was taller than the other, and the charts in the smaller pile were put into the larger stack after being read and the day's report was entered. Not being schooled in writing or reading, Etta stood and wondered why a person would scratch on paper and leave black marks on it. Many years earlier, she had seen Hubbard do something similar whenever Indian hunters brought in pelts. Francis, having been schooled, knew what the man was doing.

"Excuse me. Me and my wife are here to see our son, John Bergeron."

The dragoon finally looked up from his papers, not even realizing that Etta and Francis had come in. "John Bergeron, did you say?" He thumbed through the charts on the desk and said, "Here it is. You will need to talk to Colonel Pugsley first." Motioning to the two empty chairs that were beside the door, he continued, "Please take a seat. I'll go get him."

Etta and Francis sat down, not even speaking but staring at the floor. Finally, Francis lifted his head and noticed signs above the single doors that flanked the dragoon's desk. One of the signs read "Hospital Ward." "Bat must be in there," he whispered into Etta's ear.

Just then, the door on the other side of the desk opened. An officer and the sergeant appeared. Pointing in the direction of Etta and Francis, the sergeant said, "Mr. and Mrs. Bergeron, Sir."

Approaching Etta and Francis who by now were apprehensively standing, the officer spoke, "Mr. and Mrs. Bergeron? I'm Colonel Pugsley, the post surgeon. Thanks for coming. Sergeant Willis told me that you are here to see your son, John Bergeron."

"Yes!" blurted Francis. "How is he? What happened?"

"Sit down please," said Colonel Pugsley as he pulled up an empty chair. Pulling out a cigar, he offered it to Francis and asked, "Smoke?"

Francis shook his head and said, "Not now."

Lighting up the cigar, Colonel Pugsley said, "I just saw John. He's resting and doing as good as we can expect considering his wounds."

"What exactly happened?" implored Etta.

"About all we know is that he was ambushed and injured," added Francis.

"I fully understand your concern," answered Colonel Pugsley. "He and another scout — Wesley Lewis — he just left — were on patrol — out scouting when your son was ambushed by three Pawnees down by Council Grove . John was shot — took a bullet in the chest. He fell off his horse, and one Pawnee jumped him — cut his throat and was just about to scalp him when Lewis — Lewis came to his rescue. He killed the one who was on top of your son and fought off the other two."

"The shot went clean through so there's no ball in him

— just a nasty wound. Good thing the cut on his throat wasn't any deeper. The cut just missed his jugular vein. If it had been cut, he would have bled out — like a stuck hog. The knife wound on his neck should heal in about three weeks. Don't know how long it will take for him to recover from the gunshot wound. We cleaned out the chest wound the best we could — mainly pulled out bits of cloth that came from his blouse. Now we are trying to keep the wound clean, but I hope he doesn't get an infection. The worst would be gangrene or tetanus. We'll just have to pray and wait. I wish that we could do something for his pain."

Worriedly Etta asked, "Can we see him?"

"Yes, follow me." Colonel Pugsley, still puffing his cigar, led Etta and Francis into the hospital ward. It was a relatively small room with sunlight filtering through the side windows. Its brightness revealed a row of six beds on either side of a center aisle. The doctor turned to Etta and Francis and said, "John is in the fifth bed on your right. He'll be able to talk to you, but don't stay too long. He needs lots of rest. If you want to see me afterwards, Sergeant Willis will know where to find me."

Etta and Francis walked up to the bed where Bat was lying and looked down at him. Bloody bandaging covered his chest where he had been shot and the left side of his neck where he had sustained the serious knife wound. Etta, surfacing her inner strength, held back her tears and whispered into his ear, "*Bozhow*." Francis had to turn aside to conceal his emotions. After a few moments of silence, Bat opened his eyes. Upon seeing his parents, he managed a slight smile and returned his mother's hello. Etta reached down and grasped Bat's hand.

27 – Walked All the Way

"I think the children are glad to finally have a school in Louisville!" hollered Francis as he climbed out of bed. Etta was in her kitchen preparing breakfast and yelled back, "I don't know if they like havin' a school here as much as being able to stay home. I know that Matilda and Catherine don't like stayin' at the mission boardin' school in St. Mary's! Don't know 'bout Charles. I know I missed him when he was away! Met the teacher yet?" "Yes!" Francis said as he came out of the bedroom pulling up his suspenders, "Miss Holloway."

"Now that the children are home, maybe they'll help me plan goin' back to Illinois for a visit," said Etta as she ladled up a scoop of mush for Francis.

"I remember you said Phoebe wanted you to come back and visit the last time you saw her," said Francis as he picked up and stared into his coffee cup. "Mind if I go with you?"

The question caught Etta by surprise just as she was sitting down to eat her breakfast. Astonished, she said, "I didn't think you ever wanted to go back! What changed your mind?"

"Don't know. Guess that I would like to see Sid. I also heard that quite a few Bergeron's are living around Kankakee. They might know something about my family in Canada. Only thing I know is that some of them moved down to Vermont near Lake Champlain. Also, problems with the War are starting to come into Kansas. Guess they have been here for a long time — lots of shootings — people around here just didn't call it war. Anyway, gettin' out of here now might be a good idea. We probably should go across Iowa."

"Not take a river boat?"

"No! Missouri is filled with red necks. River boatin' to St. Louis is too dangerous."

"It'll take several moons or months, as you call them, to go and come if we don't go by boat."

"I already figured that," replied Francis.

"Who's gonna do the field work and take care of the animals?" questioned Etta.

"I already thought about that," answered Francis as he swirled his morning cup of coffee. "Bat's not completely healed, but he's strong enough now to do the work. I know that. At least his mending will keep him out of the Union Army. I've already talked to him. Besides, he wants to stay home. I think that Miss Holloway might have something to do with his wanting to stay home."

****

Etta and Phoebe stood on the banks of the Pickamick River while their children romped in the nearby groves of sugar maple and oak trees. All of them had ridden down from Momence in Phoebe's buggy so Etta could show Phoebe and the children where her village was when she was a child. Francis was not with them. He stayed behind to visit with Sid at his farm in Momence.

"See that little town across the river? It's Buncombe. That's where my tribal village used to be. We later moved a little east on this side of the river," said Etta somewhat misty-eyed. "My mother is buried along this river — not sure where anymore. I was only about fourteen when she made me go live with Hubbard. I didn't know any different then. He took me to Danville. We had a baby girl — she died there." To Phoebe, it seemed as if Etta was in a trance, re-living her life.

When the sun passed its noon-time position, Etta

hollered for Matilda, Catherine and Charles, "Children, time for us to go! Auntie Phoebe needs to go back. We'll go on to Indiana. I want to see if I can find some old friends there."

When Matilda saw Phoebe and her two children get in her buggy and start down Hubbard's Trail, as it was known locally, she asked Etta in a concerned voice, "How we gonna get there?"

"Walk," said Etta in a presumptive tone.

Matilda clinched her lower jaw and stuck out her lips as a sign of disgust.

"How long do we have to walk?" asked Catherine as they crossed the Illinois-Indiana line.

"Not much farther — I hope."

****

Etta and her children walked along a dusty road that followed along the Pickamick River into Newton County, Indiana. She inquired of the few people who were met along the way if they knew where the Todd's lived. Most people ignored her. Some shrugged their shoulders and kept on their way. When Etta was just about ready to give up her quest, she encountered a balding gentleman who told her how to get to the Todd farm.

After he gave Etta directions to the Todd's he said, "Perhaps you should know that Elbert — did you know him? — died last month. I think his widow, Sarah, is home now. She went to see her sister, over in Logansport, after Elbert passed away. I'm going that way so you and the young'uns can ride if you want to."

After Etta and her children got into the stranger's buggy, he introduced himself. "I'm Mr. Jay Hubbard. Come here shortly after my cousin, Gurdon, did. He and his wife, Watchekee, I think, took off and went down to Danville, Illinois. They didn't stay together. About that time, he quit the tradin' and moved up to Chicago."

Etta cringed. She simply introduced herself as Mrs. Bergeron.

"Whatcha' doing in these parts? Don't take offense, but you Indian? Used to be lots of Potawatomi in these areas, but they all left." His steady stream of questions interspersed with comments gave Etta little opportunity to say anything. Actually, she was glad.

"Whoa!" commanded Jay as he stopped his buggy in front of a small, white farm house. "This is Sarah's place. She should be home. Saw her this mornin'."

"Thank you," said Etta as she climbed out of Jay's buggy. The children were fast asleep and had to be shaken awake in order for Etta to get them to follow her.

As Etta and her children were making their way to the front of Sarah's house, a shaggy dog viciously began barking. Alerted by the noise, a late teen-aged boy walked around the corner of the house to see what had riled up the dog.

Seeing Etta and her children, he said, "Don't mind him. You here to see Miss Sarah? I'll get'er for you." All the while he kept looking at Catherine. In response, she blushed and impishly smiled. He knocked on the front door after walking up to porch and hollered, "Mrs. Todd, you've got company!" Turning to Etta, he said, "Excuse me, please. I've got to milk the cow." While scampering off the porch, he looked at Catherine in such a way that caused her to blush again.

A gray-haired lady in her late sixties appeared in the doorway wearing a black mourning dress. Looking through the screen door, her face was expressionless, although her slightly reddened eyes told Etta that she had been crying. As her eyes began to focus on the face of her visitor, she raised her hand to her mouth and said in disbelief, "Oh, my god! Watchekee!"

Etta graciously accepted Sarah's invitation to have supper with her and the night's lodging. At supper, Sarah looked at the children and said, "Your mother helped me and Elbert get through our first winter here. We were living in Illinois then. We had come from Ohio. The snow was really deep. Oh! It was really cold. Probably wouldn't have survived if your mother hadn't helped us."

Changing the subject to get the attention off her, Etta asked, "Who's the boy who met us in the yard?"

"Michael Melot. He prefers to be called Joe. Anyway, he's my hired hand. Elbert hired him last summer. Don't know how long I'll keep him 'cause I'm thinking of selling this place and moving over to Middleport. It's in Illinois. You know the place?"

"Of course. In fact, that's where I'm to meet Mr. Bergeron in a few days. We'll be going back to Louisville, Kansas, then."

****

"Your father should be here soon," Etta said to her fidgety children. "Play a game of who can see him first."

"Where?" asked Catherine.

Pointing her lips northeast, Etta said, "Down that road. Take Charles with you while I look around."

Much to Etta's surprise, Francis showed up with all the children, not in his buggy but in Sid's. Phoebe was with them.

"I wanted to give you a proper good-bye. When I left the other day, I thought I would never see you again. Well, I sorta have — now."

Sid looked at Francis, elbowed him and said, "Tell her!"

"Tell me what?" asked Etta curiously.

"We don't have a buggy anymore."

"What?"

"Some Union soldiers took it and our horses. Said they needed them for the War. I protested. I said me and my family needed our rig to get back to Kansas. They laughed and said, 'Walk!'"

****

Hank came out of the stage coach house fuming. "What's wrong?" asked Francis. "I can't get any more horses to run my stage coaches! Some guy from Fort Riley took my last ones. Be glad when this war gets over."

"I know what you mean. Me and Etta and the children had to walk here from Illinois. We got back last week."

"You did what?"

"We walked from Illinois — all the way! Our buggy and horses were taken by some Blue Coats even before we got started. We didn't have much money with us so we walked. Yep — all the way!"

"Then you mustn't been around when Quantrill burned Lawrence," said Hank. Talking about the massacre made Hank calm down about his horses being commandeered. "I still can't believe you walked from Illinois."

"I heard about the trouble in Lawrence when me and Etta got close to Topeka on our way home. I gotta go. Here comes Bat."

"Before you go, I got something to tell you."

"What's that?"

"A couple of young fellas came in on the stage from St. Mary's — yesterday before I was shut down — one wanted to know if I knew where yu'awl lived."

"Did you catch their names?"

"Joe and Glaude Melot accordin' to the passenger list. I took them to be brothers."

"Did they say anything about being from Indiana?"

"By gosh, they did. Do you know them?"

"No, but Etta met one to them when she went to visit a friend in Indiana. Based on what she told me, I think I know why he's come here. Don't know anything about the other one."

28 – Mr. Bergeron! Mr. Bergeron!

Scarcely one year after walking from Illinois, Francis did a double-take when he saw a flash of red hair in his defending unit. As a volunteer Union infantryman, he was entrenched at Westport, Missouri, preparing to fight the Confederates, under the command of Major General Sterling Price, that were threatening to seize the town. Francis volunteered for duty, in part, to appease Etta. She and the other Potawatomi in Kansas were growing concerned the Confederates and in particular, Price's military campaign in Missouri, would adversely affect them. Quantrill's destruction of and massacre in Lawrence the previous year precipitated her anxiousness.

After the battle in which Price's forces were defeated, Francis and the other Union soldiers took a well deserved rest although they remained alert to a possible counter attack. Francis used the interlude as an opportunity to seek out the red-haired man that he glimpsed just before guns and cannons opened fire. Now, it was quiet, and the smell of burnt gun powder filled the air. It came from the haze that hung over the battle field. Francis hoped the man he was looking for would not be among the dead or wounded. He searched for twenty minutes. — Then, next to a tree stump, twisted and splintered from the ravages of war, Francis spotted him. He was kneeling on the red-stained grass, cradling the head of a mortally wounded friend whom he was trying to comfort.

Just as the wounded soldier took a final, gasping breath, Francis asked "ARE YOU WESLEY LEWIS?" An artillery barrage had ruptured his ear drums. The red-haired man laid down the head of his dead friend. Standing up and facing Francis, he replied, "YES." He too had lost much of his hearing and also had ringing in his ears.

"SPEAK LOUDER, I CAN'T HEAR VERY GOOD!" shouted Francis. While the two men talked loudly, they watched the wounded being loaded onto litters and shoved aboard medical wagons. "YES! I'M WESLEY. HOW DID YOU KNOW?" Wesley answered but kept his eyes on the wounded. "WHERE ARE THEY TAKING THEM?" His concern seemed to be directed to no one in particular.

"I HEARD SOMEONE SAY THIS MORNING THAT SOME OF THE WOUNDED WOULD BE TAKEN TO FORT RILEY. THAT'S WHERE I THINK I SAW YOU! COLONEL PUGSLEY THERE TOLD ME YOU SAVED MY SON'S LIFE!" said Francis.

Wesley turned to the stranger. In astonishment, he replied, "BAT? YOU'RE HIS FATHER? HOW'S HE DOING?"

"FINE — THANKS TO YOU! HE SEEMS TO BE HEALED, BUT CAN'T GET ALL HIS STRENGTH BACK! I KNOW HE'D BE GLAD TO SEE YOU. DON'T KNOW WHEN WE'LL GET MUSTERED OUT, BUT WHEN WE DO, HOPE YOU CAN STOP BY! HE'S LIVING AT HOME WITH ME AND MY WIFE, ETTA!"

"WHERE'S THAT?" asked Wesley

"LOUISVILLE."

Francis took a swig of water from his canteen. Wesley reached for his canteen also, but it was empty. It had a bullet hole in it. Wesley graciously accepted a drink from Francis. Both men suddenly realized what had happened, and Wesley shouted, "DIDN'T KNOW THAT IT GOT SHOT! A BULLET MUST HAVE GONE THROUGH IT. I FELT MY TROUSERS GETTING WET DURING THE FIGHTING! THOUGHT I HAD PEED! GOSH, I WAS SCARED!" Francis nodded his head as a way of letting Wesley know that the fighting frightened him too.

"You two! Get a litter and help load up the wounded!" ordered Major General Dietzler, commander of the Kansas Militia. Francis and Wesley continued talking to each other. The commanding officer became increasingly incensed, not knowing why he was being ignored. He finally got their attention and made them understand what he ordered them to do.

Francis and Wesley did not relish obeying the general's orders. In order to determine if a soldier was injured or dead it meant looking at each fallen man. Sometimes, they had to turn the casualty over. The task was gruesome. Suddenly, Francis stopped and turned pale. Wesley, not understanding what had affected Francis, shouted "WHAT'S WRONG?"

Francis starring at a dead man stammered, "K-K-KAH-DAH-DAS! HOW AM I GONNA TELL OLIVIE?'

****

Several Potawatomi were stationed at Fort Row, a small Union outpost in southeastern Kansas. The fort's only significant action during the Civil War was its attempt to care for and accommodate the Creeks who had fled north from Indian Territory to show their allegiance to the Unionists. Two in the Potawatomi contingent were Moke-je-win and Gah-gha-dmo. They were at nearby Delaware Springs late one afternoon while off duty, sharing stories told to them by their parents about the long, forced removal from Indiana some twenty-six years earlier. They were born after the removal so had no hardships of their own to recount about the tragedy. In the middle of one of the stories, splashing was heard coming from the Verdigris River. The nature of the splashing told the two men that horses were moving rapidly. Major General Price and his men, at least what was left of them, were retreating from the victorious Union army. They were circumventing Fort Smith in northwestern Arkansas. The safety they sought was farther south in Arkansas. Consequently, the Confederates chose to flee southwest on the West Shawnee Trail to central, unorganized Indian Territory. There, they crossed the North Canadian River and continued south on the Arbuckle Wagon Road before swinging east after fording the South Canadian River.

"Well, I'll be," said Moke-je-win. "Them's Rebs!" He stood and looked in astonishment. Soon, horse-mounted Union soldiers appeared, pursing the remnants of Price's army.

****

Joe Melot had trouble finding work after arriving in Louisville, or at least steady work. He finally rode over to Fort Riley seeking to enlist in the army. There, because of his age, he was deemed too young for military duty. However, the commissary officer hired him to procure meat for the fort's troops. He unofficially became known as the "Little Herder" because he herded in small numbers of steers and occasionally hogs to the fort where they were butchered. In this capacity, he drove in 'meat' from as far away as St. Mary's. The trips in that direction took him through Louisville. He took the opportunity when passing through or near the town to frequently inquire if the Bergeron's had any stock to sell. The frequency of his inquiries increased and led to dinner invitations. Joe's so-called business ventures gave him valued moments to visit his primary focus, Catherine. Somehow, Catherine knew when to expect Joe because she would not put on a work dress on that day and refrained from getting dirty. It didn't take Etta and Francis long to figure out Joe's intentions.

****

Opening the gate, Joe re-mounted his riding mule and began herding twenty-three steers into the pen beside Fort

Riley's butchering shed. As he got the last of the steers into the pen, he began seeing a long line of various types of single-horse drawn wagons, some two-wheeled, others four-wheeled. Many were covered with canvas and resembled moving, white rectangular boxes. All had been assembled or commandeered for the singular purpose of transporting those wounded in the battle at Westport to Fort Riley.

Joe ran over to the fort's main gate and vomited when he saw the human carnage carried in the wagons. Quickly, each wagon was unloaded of its bloody cargo as it pulled up to the fort's hospital and the newly erected tents that surrounded it. Medical aides stood nearby and determined if the wounded were to be treated for non-gunshot wounds or gunshots or knife stabbings. The blood-stained corpses of the men who died on the way to Fort Riley from Westport were laid in rows on the ground next to where the wagons were coming in. To Joe, the stacked bodies resembled cords of firewood. He was witnessing a scene that he never imagined he would ever see.

"Mr. Bergeron! Mr. Bergeron!" shouted Joe as one of the wagons passed before him. Francis kept his concentration on the medical wagon in front of him. Besides he loss of hearing kept him hearing Joe.

"You, over there, help get the wounded out of the wagons!" barked one of the medical aides. Joe realized that the order was directed at him and unhesitatingly began the daunting task of being a litter bearer. Being close to the victims of war, Joe could smell the distinctive odor of gangrenous infection that already had set in. According to the judgment of the medical aide looking at the condition of a wounded soldier, Joe was directed to carry the wounded soldier to either a general tent or an amputation tent.

Francis waited with bowed head as his wagon was unloaded. He then got off his wagon as a private from the fort drove it over to the line of other empty wagons. Soldiers with mops, scrub brushes and water already were cleaning them.

Francis walked over to the barrels of drinking water that awaited the drivers of the wagons. He ladled a drink and sat down in the shade of the only tree in the vicinity of the hospital. As he sat, Wesley came up and joined him. He said, "NEVER THOUGHT I WOULD SEE THIS PLACE AGAIN. I RESIGNED FROM SCOUTING AFTER SEEING THAT BAT WAS SAFE IN THE HOSPITAL AND STARTED DRIVIN' ON THE SANTA FE TRAIL. "

Other drivers, because of Wesley's loud voice, looked around thinking that the comment might have been directed at them. Francis knew differently. Piercing screams already were filling the air. The cries were coming from the makeshift amputation tent. Ruptured ear drums or not, Francis and Wesley could hear them. As Francis heard the cries of agony, he thought to himself, "*At least Bat came out whole!*"

29 – K-K-K-Kate!

Splitting firewood in preparation for the coming winter was not Bat's preferred chore on the farm. Yet, he knew that it had to be done. It meant survival. After all, he remembered, the holy water froze last winter at St. Mary's. As Bat raised his splitting axe, he caught sight of a familiar figure approaching the house. "Father!" he shouted and dropped his axe.

Etta came out of the house when she heard Bat. At first, she strained her eyes and shaded them to get a better look. When she realized that her prayers had been answered, she rushed off the porch and into the arms of the one she had so learned to love. Catherine and Charles were at school where Miss Holloway taught and did not get to share the exuberance being expressed that day on the Bergeron farm. Etta had heard that the Union army was victorious at Westport, but until she saw Francis that early November day she did not know he had survived the battle.

"I had no idea that you would be home so soon — if ever," Etta said teary-eyed.

"WHAT DID YOU SAY?" replied Francis. He pointed to his ears indicating that it was difficult for him to hear. Etta was taken aback at her husband's behavior. Finally, Francis made a scribbling motion to Bat. Understanding his father wanted to write something, Bat ran into the house and came out with a pencil and a piece of paper. Francis quickly wrote a message and gave it to Bat, knowing Etta did not read. Turning to his mother, Bat explained, "Father's ears are bad. The sound of the fighting made it hard for him to hear. Dr. Pugsley at Fort Riley said his bad ears would get better in a few weeks. Because he can't hear very good, the army told him to go home."

Understanding Bat's explanation, Etta smiled. She then took Francis's hand, looked up at him and led him into the house. "We need to get you out of this cold wind." As they entered the house, Matilda came home from taking care of her new niece so Olivie could rest. Hugging her father and welcoming him home, she too did not understand his quietness until Bat told her what had happened to their father and to her husband, Kah-dah-das.

Catherine and Charles come bounding in the front door, cold from their long walk home from school. "Shh. Quiet. Your father's sleeping," said Etta while holding her index finger next to her lips. They grinned and silently clapped their hands in excitement upon learning that their father was safely home.

Before Etta extinguished the oil lamps for the evening, she noticed that Francis was cupping his hands over his ears. His movements told Etta that Francis in pain. She quickly went out of the bedroom and soon returned carrying a small jar of yellowish water. "POTAWATOMI MEDICINE," she said loud enough for Francis to hear. Motioning for Francis to lie on his side, she began spooning the liquid, first into his right ear, and then his left when he turned over. It was warm and soothing.

"WHAT IS IT?" Francis asked.
"MY WATER."

****

"Morning, Joe. Checkn' to see if we have any steers? No. Want some coffee? Kinda cold today. Let's go inside," said Francis as he opened the door for the 'Little Herder.'

As Francis and Joe stomped the first season's snow off their boots and hung up their heavy coats, Etta cheerfully greeted Joe, "*Bozhow.*" Joe knew enough Potawatomi to recognize the greeting and replied similarly. His response made Etta smile.

"Etta, please get me and Joe some coffee." After Etta poured coffee into their cups, Francis said, "We don't have anything to sell. I butchered our last yearling steer early this mornin'. It and the hog are hangin' in the smoke house. We'll have just enough meat to get us through the winter. Come spring, we'll have something for you."

"Makes sense," replied Joe. Francis noticed that Joe was quite nervous and suspected that he had come to talk about other matters. "*He'll spit it out,*" thought Francis, laughing inside. Joe wasn't ready to talk yet about what really was on his mind and quickly launched into another subject. "People at Fort Riley told me that you lost your hearing because of a cannon blast at the fight in Westport. You must be alright now. I mean you speak about normal now."

"I still have some trouble, but I'm gettin' along pretty good. I even could talk fairly good — and hear too — when Wesley Lewis — don't think you know him — came by last week."

"Who's Wesley Lewis?"

"He's the one who saved Bat, and we fought together at Westport. After we won the battle, I invited him to stop by someday to visit. He did, but we didn't get much visiting done. He didn't say much to Bat either."

"How come?"

"Him and Matilda got to talking. I guess he forgot why he came!" laughed Francis as he took a sip of his coffee.

Joe continued to squirm. Francis continued to watch Joe's uneasiness. As beads of perspiration began to appear on Joe's forehead, Francis thought, "*He's soon gonna speak his real business.*" After several agonizing moments, Joe finally asked, "Mr. Bergeron, c-c-can I marry your daughter?"

"Which one?" Francis answered coyly.

Joe became flustered and stammered, "K-K-K-Kate!"

30 – Talk With Moke-je-win

Joe learned through his contacts that the Bourbonnais family near St. Mary's had several head of steers that he might be able to buy for Fort Riley. He thought that if he could get them and the seven that Archange had for him, a trip east would be profitable. Archange, Kate's half-sister, had proven to be a good source for procurements.

After successively negotiating and getting twenty-one steers from the Bourbonnias's, Joe drove his herd towards Archange's place. Because of the lateness in the afternoon and the cold that was setting in, Archange invited Joe to spend the evening before heading back to Fort Riley.

"There's enough room in the corral for the steers that you brought. Fetch some feed and water for them. There's straw in the barn for beddin'. Stayin' will give you a chance to meet my husband, Moke-je-win. He went to see the Fathers at the mission. Should be back before it gets dark," she chatted.

Joe readily accepted Archange's invitation. Because of his dating Kate, he essentially had become a family member. *"After supper,"* he excitedly thought, *"I can tell her that Francis agreed to lettin' me marry Kate!"*

Pulling up a chair by the fireplace, Joe belched and joined Archange and Moke-je-win who already was in front of it warming his feet. Joe used the opportunity to tell them of the talk he had with Francis two days earlier.

"When you gonna get married? Kate's but fifteen — just turned fifteen I was told," said Moke-je-win picking up and cleaning out his clay pipe with his knife.

"Francis and me talked about that. Told him that Kate

and me had talked about the same thing and want to wait 'til April.

"April? She'll still be fifteen."

"No! Not this coming April, but April the next year."

"Hmm!" responded Moke-je-win as he shook burnt tobacco from his pipe and threw a handful of blackened pieces into the fire that was starting to dwindle. "Archange, hand me a couple of pieces of wood!" As Moke-je-win threw the wood onto the fire and stoked it, he added, "Figured out where you gonna live?"

"Not sure. Francis offered a place. I told him me and Kate would talk about it."

"Where's that?" asked Archange sitting next to Moke-je-win and rocking her young daughter by her first husband.

"It's the cabin that Francis and Bat moved to the Lasley claim for Father Duerinck. It'll be empty 'cause Father is moving out 'bout the time me and Kate plan to get married."

"Still gonna go around and get cattle for the fort?" asked Moke-je-win.

"'Til I get somethin' better."

****

"Don't know why it was necessary for me to get citizenship," said Kate while she and Joe ate their meager evening meal.

"At least now that you have it, you can get an allotment of land. Isn't that what the 1863 Treaty said?" answered Joe reaching for another piece of cornbread.

"The allotment, I was told, only would be for eighty acres of land. Sure, father is lettin' us stay in this here cabin, but we can't eat the land when we get it. Maybe we should sell the allotment before we lose it," lamented Kate.

"How's that?" asked Joe.

"Heard some of our people say that they lost their

allotments 'cause they forgot to pay taxes. Government took their allotments away. If you see people looking around for work, it's probably 'cause they lost their land and got nothing to farm. Some of them are becoming drifters and alcoholics."

"Perhaps we could use the allotment to get a loan from the bank in St. Mary's. I know that my job at the fort doesn't pay much. A loan would help us," said Joe as he finished the cornbread and drank the last of his coffee.

"Don't like the idea of a loan."

"Why not?" queried Joe.

"Learned in school that a loan gotta be paid back. There's also something called interest. Don't understand it, but lots of money is owed. Somehow the bank and the railroad keep getting' more and more of the land that is lost. What we gonna do?"

"Don't know."

****

Joe was troubled when he overheard some of the soldiers at Fort Riley boasting about killing Cheyenne men, women and children and destroying their villages in western Unorganized Indian Territory. He knew that the Cheyenne there were friendly to the government. The low pay of his job and the atrocities that he heard were taking away his incentive to work for the fort. In addition, Kate was growing increasingly dissatisfied with the long absences required by Joe's work.

Joe's grumbling about his job became more and more apparent to family members. Kate confided with Etta about Joe's growing discontentment, and Joe directly expressed his feelings to Francis and to a degree with Archange's husband, Moke-je-win.

During one his visits with Moke-je-win, Joe got a new idea after Moke-je-win told him about an experience that he had when serving at Fort Row. After driving his herd to Fort Riley, Joe rode home and shared his plan with Kate. It was late when Joe arrived home, but he unsaddled his horse and turned it loose in the pen as usual. Everything was normal in Kate's eyes. However, Joe's whistling as he came into the cabin wasn't. It caused Kate to say, "You sound especially happy." "Happy?" Joe replied, "I just quit!" "What?" cried Kate. "Just like that? Did you get another job?"

"Let me explain what I learned from Moke-je-win and tell you what I think we should do. When Moke-je-win was at Fort Row, you know southeast of us, he saw a bunch of Confederates. It turns out they was runnin' from getting' their butts whipped at Westport — that's where your father fought. They got chased clear down into Indian Territory by Union soldiers. A few weeks later the Union men returned and stayed at Fort Row for a couple of days. Moke-je-win got to talkin' with one of the soldiers, even took care of his horse. It was really worn out. Anyway, the chase stopped after the Rebs got across what he — the Union soldier — called the South Canadian River. The cavalry turned around there and camped for a couple of days at a valley overlookin' a little river they called Pond Creek. The soldier told Moke-je-win that no one was livin' there, only lush prairie and lots of timber."

Sitting down, Kate looked at Joe and emotionally asked, "What are you getting at? Are you saying we should move there?"

31 – Journey's Over

It happened fast, much faster than Kate had anticipated. The sale of Kate's allotment southwest of Louis Vieux's bridge brought sufficient funds for her and Joe to purchase a wagon. It was for moving to the area described to Moke-je-win by the Union soldier who had helped chase Major General Price and his men across the South Canadian River.

Joe used a team of borrowed draft horses to pull the wagon to the cabin where he and Kate lived. After Joe returned the horses to Hank's Livery, Kate sarcastically asked, "What now?" Joe shrugged his shoulders. While Kate and Joe stood looking dejectedly at their unmovable wagon, they heard a familiar voice and turned around.

"Haw!" commanded Francis to a pair of oxen yoked together. Dutifully, they turned left and into the cabin yard. Stopping by the wagon, Francis said, "Me and Etta figured that you could use somethin'' to pull the wagon and help break some sod." Etta and Kate's siblings soon arrived in a buggy, and upon arriving, started loading the wagon. Although not in favor of seeing their daughter move, he and Etta nevertheless had come to help. Etta carried loads to the wagon, but Francis noticed her tiring out easily and breathing hard as if she was trying to catch her breath.

Kate's eyes welled up when the last load was put on the wagon. "*Mgwetch*," she said. "I want to thank you too," gratefully added Joe.

Looking around, Kate saw that her two-year old son, Ltl' Joe, had wandered away teetering after a cat that was scurrying alongside the cabin that she and Joe were preparing to leave. Hurrying after Ltl' Joe, Kate quickly caught up with him. Scooping him up amidst his squeals of protest, Kate bought him back and put him in the wagon.

Tearfully, the good-byes were said. After Joe tied his horse and milk cow to the back of the wagon, he and Kate started their journey to find the lush prairie valley north of the South Canadian River. They headed southwest along the Military Road and spent the first night camped near Manhattan. The next morning Kate and Joe plodded past Fort Riley, eventually got on the treeless Chisholm Trail at Abilene and headed south.

Along the way, Joe told Kate more about the place where they were going. "It used to be occupied by the Seminoles who were forced out of Florida. However, they were shoved east of where we're goin' 'cause they fought with the Confederates. Still, they'll be the closest neighbors east of us. Chickasaws are south — on the other side of South Canadian River. So-called 'uncivilized' Indians, the Comanche and Cheyenne, west. Expect to see some Shawnees. They're around North Canadian River — about thirty miles north of where we're gonna be."

"Will we see any of them along the way?" asked Kate.

"Maybe. We'll go south on this here Chisholm Trail 'til we get on the Cheyenne Agency Road just after we cross the North Canadian west of the Shawnees. See here on this map," said Joe, as he pointed out the area to Kate on the military map that he had gotten just before leaving Louisville. "The agency road will take us through the Cross Timbers to the Arbuckle Wagon Road. Then we'll go south for 'bout a day."

"Why we goin' this way instead of down from Topeka towards Delaware Springs and Fort Now where Moke-je-win was? Accordin' to the map we got, it's shorter that way," jabbered Kate as she studied the routes.

"It might be shorter through eastern Kansas and hookin' up with the West Shawnee Trail in Indian Territory.

A couple of years ago, we would've gone down that way, but this way's faster. The country's flatter west of the Flint Hills, and there're fewer rivers to cross. Some men did a good job of runnin' Jesse Chisholm's trade route from the Arkansas River north to Abilene. His old trail mainly was used before for tradin' in Indian Territory," explained Joe. "I heard 'bout it shortly before I quit my job at Fort Riley. Probably a good thing I quit 'cause I would've soon lost my job anyway."

"How's that?" queried Kate.

"Cattle from Texas, lots of them, started comin' up the Chisholm Trail last year. At Abilene they got loaded onto the new Atchison, Topeka and Santa Fe Railway and sold out east. The railway goes right by Fort Riley. The fort now can get all the beef it needs. No longer needs the work that I did."

As they lumbered along, Kate pondered what her mother told her about the removals of the Potawatomi from Illinois and Indiana. *"Everyone always is being made to start over in strange places. Hardships never seem to stop,"* she thought.

****

Trees and brush became evident as Kate and Joe began travelling through Cross Timbers, a band of very dense forest and brush that extended from central Texas to southeastern Kansas. Even though timbered vegetation was evident, Kate was becoming more and more apprehensive about the move.

Turning south onto the Arbuckle Wagon Road and crossing Little River, Kate and Joe stopped and camped for the night. Early the next morning, Joe said, "According to this rough map, we need to go south about another fifteen miles and then turn west. It'll be rough then. Expect that it'll take us 'bout two more days to get where we want to go."

"*Good*!" thought Kate. Looking at the terrain she remarked, "How much redder can the dirt get? Sure we can grow anything here?" Joe didn't answer. Kate's demeanor was soured by a fitful night of sleep that was punctuated by the piercing scream of a bobcat prowling the hills overlooking Little River.

****

Kate raised her head when Joe commanded the oxen to stop and felt the wagon lurch slightly forward. She had been trying to doze but the wagon's bouncing over rocks and jerking after leaving the Arbuckle Wagon Road made any attempt to rest unsuccessful. Looking up, she was on a ridge strewn with chunks of red sandstone and clumps of grass. The rest of the landscape was dotted with junipers, oaks, and pecan trees. But a green valley lay below. Just as described, it was covered with a bounty of swaying prairie grasses. Scanning the distant southern border of the valley she saw a string of trees. Pointing with her pursed kips, Kate asked, "What's way over there?" "According to the map, a stream — it must be Pond Creek," answered Joe.

Joe, riding the wagon's brakes, carefully descended the hillside and stopped when he reached verdant grasses below. There, he jumped off the wagon and unyoked the oxen. Untying the rest of his livestock from the rear of the wagon, he took all of the animals, tied them together and put them in the shade of a large oak tree. "Journey's over!" he said as he gave his riding horse that had been tied to and trailing the wagon a playful pat on its haunches.

Joe and Kate took a drink of water from the barrel strapped to the side of the wagon and then walked around trying to determine the best location for their future cabin. "I want to look out over the valley," she said. "Expect that means we should find a spot along the south side of the hill we just came down — about where we stand," replied Joe as he nodded his head in agreement. Twisting around and waving his hand to the hills behind him, he added, "This spot also will protect us from any north winds come winter."

"We'll start the cabin and sod breakin' tomorrow. Tonight we'll rest," said Joe. Looking back at the wagon, Joe noticed Kate had put a blanket under it and already was asleep with Ltl' Joe safely beside her. Travel weariness had overcome her. Joe gazed down at his family and smiled. Spitting out his tobacco juice, he quietly said, "At least she and Ltl' Joe won't have to put up with anymore wagon bounces."

****

Kate had ambivalent thoughts about the place that she and Joe were developing as their new home. She liked the isolation, but establishing it was much harder than she had thought it would be. Joe was startled when Kate yelled, "When are we gonna get started with the cabin?" "Gotta break enough sod so we can grow some food for ourselves and the animals if we want to get though the winter!" he yelled back.

Tensions were mounting. Kate was getting tired of sleeping under the wagon, and life was made very miserable when rain storms, accompanied by high winds and flashes of lightening, roared through the valley. Joe, meanwhile, got his crops planted and dug a well. For several months, he also cut and shaped logs for the dog-trot cabin. Kate helped Joe pull up and place the logs. During the time that Joe was working his crops, Kate and Ltl' Joe gathered pieces of red sandstone rocks for chinking the seams of the cabin. The finished cabin was similar to Archange's one-story structure in Kansas: fifteen by eighteen feet rooms on each side of the dog-trot. One room was for cooking and eating and the other for sleeping with second-floor lofts for more sleeping quarters. Kate's and Joe's first night in the cabin with its distinctive red sandstone and red mud chinking did not come until after the first frost.

32 – Left Alone

"JOE!" yelled Kate. "RIDERS ARE COMING!" She shouted through a back window to Joe who was hammering on the corn crib that he was finishing. He stepped to the east side of the crib to get a better look at the men who were coming. Seeing two, unshaven men wearing a mix of old Confederate uniforms and civilian clothes made Joe uneasy. He picked up his rifle that he had propped against the cabin wall. Cradling the rifle and holding up the other hand was a sign to the approaching men that they needed to stop.

Kate and Joe had grown used to seeing 'drifters' but they never approached the cabin before. When Joe first saw the men, they were trotting their horses. They slowed their steeds to a walk when they saw Joe, but kept coming. As the men got closer, they started walking their horses in opposite directions and drew their pistols. It was an attempt to partially encircle Joe and flank him. When Joe saw this move, he raised his rifle to his shoulder but realized that he was not only outgunned but outmaneuvered and began to sweat.

Suddenly there was a loud shot! BOOM! The hat flew off the head of the rider to the right of Joe. The noise of the gunshot startled his horse, and it started bucking. Attempting to get his horse under control, the rider, with his pistol in one hand, pulled the reins hard with his free hand in an effort to get the horse's head up, but one of the reins broke. Because the rider was pulling hard, he tumbled backwards and started falling to the ground. As he fell backwards, the horse kicked out with its hind legs. One hoof caught the airborne rider on the forehead above the left eye. The kick stripped the hatless rider's skin back, and blood began streaming down his face.

Seeing what was had happened to his partner, the second rider wheeled his horse around and raced to the man who was just getting on his feet. As his partner dashed up to him, the now-bloodied man grabbed the out-stretched arm of the second drifter and was pulled onto his horse. Riding double, they raced eastward toward the Arbuckle Wagon Road and vanished.

Joe realized that Kate was the one who fired the shot that spooked the horse. Rushing to where he had heard the blast come from, he found Kate, trembling and sprawled on the ground. She was holding her right shoulder. Joe's old, long-barrel muzzle loader was beside her.

"Did I get him?" she asked looking up at Joe.

"No! But you scared them off! Must've grazed the one who fell off his horse. His head was bleedin'! What's wrong? Hurt your shoulder?"

"When I shot, the gun knocked me backwards!" Kate said while rubbing her shoulder.

Helping Kate stand up and brushing dirt off her skirt and the back of her blouse, Joe said, "Muzzle loaders like mine have quite a kick. One's got to hold it snug up against the shoulder before shootin'." Joe reached down and picked up the gun. "Didn't know that you knew how to fire it," he remarked. "My mother taught me some years ago to load it and shoot it," Kate answered.

****

Two weeks later when signs of autumn were unmistakable, Joe, as he was eating his evening meal, said, "I need to go to Cheyenne Agency and get some supplies to see us through the winter. If I leave first thing in the mornin', I should be back in 'bout five days. I'll hitch up the horses to the wagon so I can go faster."

In spite of her bravery, Kate didn't like the idea of

being left alone. After all, she and Joe had been together ever since leaving Kansas. "What if the two men come back? Those uncivilized whites!" she implored.

"Shoot 'em! I'll leave my rifle with you. Keep the muzzle loader primed too. If you've got to, use it first!"

****

An early, freakish snowstorm blew up as Joe made his way back home from his trip to the Cheyenne Agency. *"Glad that I chopped some wood last week. Kate and Ltl' Joe should be warm,"* he thought as he got closer to home. Upon seeing a faint glow in his cabin's windows through the blowing snow, he snapped the harness reins and hurried his team along. *"It'll be nice to get warm."*

After arriving at the cabin and unhitching the horses, Joe quickly led them into his little barn. There, he unharnessed and wiped them down. After feeding and watering his exhausted horses, Joe headed for the cabin. Making his way to the cabin, he hunched up his buffalo overcoat and pulled down his hat to keep the falling snow from going down his neck.

Joe flung open the door, stomped the snow from his boots, and started to say, "I'm ho…." when he saw that he was facing the barrel of his muzzle loader. Brandishing the gun was Kate. She was sitting in her rocking chair facing the door with the rifle across her lap. Ltl' Joe was curled up and sleeping on the floor beside her.

"It's me!" Joe said as he held his arms over his face. His action amply shielded his face, but would not have prevented certain death if Kate had fired the gun.

Peeking through his fingers, Joe looked and saw Kate's face. It was sullen and tear-stained. Joe's emotions turned from fright to almost helplessness when Kate said, "I'm going to have another baby. I can't have it here. There's nobody to help me should I need help."

Joe, still wearing his hat and overcoat, knelt in front of her. Gently pushing the gun barrel aside, he said in a voice that trembled with an excitement that was toned with concern, "What? When you gonna have it? Whadda you mean not here? We could go to Cheyenne Agency or up to the Shawnees when the time comes!"

"No!" replied Kate. "I wanna go back to Louisville."

"Louisville? That's way back in Kansas!"

"Yes! I know. We got time. Don't think that the baby will come until next summer."

33 – Tell Me About It

Etta slowly opened and entered the front door of her little house on the south side of Wamego where she and Francis had just moved. The basket that she was carrying was filled with freshly dug prairie turnips that flourished between Wamego and Louisville. Digging them was an effort, and the task had brought Etta to the brink of exhaustion. As she turned to close the door, she dropped her basket when she caught sight of two familiar faces in a wagon that coming down the street.

"FRANCIS!"

Fearing the worst, Francis ran to the front of the house still holding the axe that he was using to clear brush. He noticed that Etta was walking in her limp-way toward the wagon that was approaching. His concern about Etta suddenly vanished when he realized the people in the wagon were Kate and Joe.

Joe stopped the wagon, but before he could set the brakes, Kate jumped to the ground and was warmly hugging and kissing her mother. Joe, meanwhile, remained in the wagon and watched the joyous homecoming. He looked up and saw Francis, who was smiling as wide as Joe could remember. Climbing off the wagon, Joe went over and hugged his father-in-law, who by now also was warmly greeting Kate.

To satisfy his curiosity, Francis asked Joe, "How did you find us?"

"We stopped in Louisville first. Mr. Langthon who now lives on your old place told us where to find you."

"Where's Ltl' Joe?" asked Etta.

Kate smiled and said, "He's in the wagon, sleepin'."

Everybody laughed as they looked into the wagon.

As they were laughing, Etta noticed Kate's stomach. Motherly and delightful seriousness overcame Etta. She wanted to reach out and put her hands on the bulge that Kate was trying to conceal with the fullness of her skirt. However, Etta's cultural ways prevented her from invading another's personal space so instead of patting Kate's stomach she cast her eyes to it and simply asked, "When?"

"I think towards the end of summer."

"Joe, get Ltl' Joe from the wagon. Let's go inside where we can sit down and visit," said Francis as he gestured toward the house.

As they were making their way to the house, Kate asked, "Is Charles home?"

"No," answered Etta. "This is the last day of school. You'll hear him hollerin' and gallopin' his horse home pretty soon. I know that Charles is excited because school is endin', but he'll really be happy when he sees you!"

****

As Kate and Joe were talking about how much they enjoyed living in the Indian Territory, Joe explained that the main reason for returning was because of Kate's desire to have someone help her with her delivery. "There are other reasons," interjected Kate. "Oh, yes," replied Joe, "the uncivilized Indians." "Don't forget the uncivilized Whites, too!" quickly added Kate.

"What do you mean?" queried Francis with a puzzled look.

Joe took the lead and said, "The supposed civilized Chickasaws aren't always so civilized. There're a few renegades among them. They sometimes came up and harassed us." Kate unhesitatingly added, "The uncivilized

Whites are 'drifters.' They used to be Confederates. Now they're lookin' for work or somethin' to steal. It got to be hard watchin' for them 'cause there was just me and Joe."

Joe started laughing when he thought of the time Kate shot off a drifter's hat and told Etta and Francis about the incident.

Family talk soon transformed into the state of the Potawatomi who had voted to get individual allotments of land. "Lots of the people here are hurting, lost their land and don't have nothing to do," said Francis as he shifted in his chair. "Lot of good citizenship has done for them," he added sarcastically.

"Kate sold her allotment. The money we got from it helped us move to the Indian Territory," commented Joe.

"Good thing you did something with it. Anyway a new treaty was signed two years ago, not too long before you and Kate left."

"I know, but never did understand it," remarked Joe.

"Me too," added Kate.

"Not all the land set aside for the Citizen Potawatomi was allotted. We got to sell what was left over. It made the Santa Fe Railway very happy."

"There's gotta to be some money from the land then. What's gonna be done with it?" asked Kate.

Francis turned and looked at her and said, "Buy a new reservation — one where we can start over. We just gotta find a way to move there once we decide where. Guess that's where I come in. I'm just talking about finding a place. How we get there is another matter."

Kate and Joe looked dumbly at each other.

Francis sensed their curiosity and added before they could ask him another question, "Me and some other men were asked by our council to go find a place where we could all move. Our delegation, guess that's what we're called, is leaving later this year, probably in December, to look at places in the Indian Territory. We're to come back and make our suggestion to Luther Palmer, the Indian Agent over at St. Mary's. You've probably been wondering if where you went would be of any interest to us. Perhaps. Tell me about it."

34 – The Exploration

The men who had been chosen to serve on the exploratory delegation looked at each other in disbelief when Mr. Palmer said, "I want your suggestion for a new reservation in the Indian Territory by the end of February. You'll have to choose some of the Cherokee land or find some other place." As Francis and the other men left the little stone agency building after their meeting with the Indian Agent, Bernard Bertrand turned around and grumbled, "How we gonna have time to look for a place for a new reservation? Palmer wants our suggestion by the end of February. It's already November, and we aren't planning to start looking until next month. We won't have time to ride there and back, especially if bad weather comes." Looking at the other delegates, he said, "Let's ride over to my house and talk about how we can to do what Mr. Palmer wants."

****

Three members of the exploratory delegation met at the Kansas Stage Coach station in Louisville as snow swirled around them. It had come from an early December storm that had swept through the Kansas River Valley during the night. Pulling up their overcoats to keep out the blowing snow and to stop their shivering, Bernard and the other two waited for the stage coach to pull in. The delegates had decided after being told of the February deadline that travelling as far as they could by stage coach would make the search within the imposed time frame a doable task.

"Where you headed?" shouted down the driver as he

pulled on the reins of his horses. They were stomping their hooves and mouthing the bits in their mouths, showing their eagerness to continue the run westward toward Fort Riley.

"Abilene and then south past Kansas!" yelled back Bernard.

The driver looked at his bundled up 'shotgun' partner and back down at Bernard. Laughing, he remarked, "South, past Kansas? You'll have to transfer to the KT Stage Coach in Abilene. Sounds like you're headed to the Indian Territory. Not much to do down there, especially this time of year. You'd have more fun goin' west to Denver. How about you other men?"

"We're all together," responded Bernard.

"Get in then! As soon as the cargo that we're to pick up gets loaded, we'll be on our way!" yelled back the driver.

****

Bernard and two other men, Joshua Clardy and Maresiuss, comprised an advance party of the six men delegated to find a new reservation area in Indian Country. The plan was for all members of the delegation to rendezvous at the Cheyenne Agency. The responsibility of the advance group was to secure six riding horses and two pack mules. Two days after arriving at the Cheyenne Agency, they waited at the agency's stage coach station for the arrival of Francis and the rest of the delegation. Chief Wiwise, the elder chosen for the delegation and who was with the group that included Francis, got off the stage and stretched. He was pleased to see that the pack mules already bore the necessary gear and supplies for the important assignment that awaited the men.

Taking the Cheyenne Agency Wagon Road, the six-member delegation, bundled against the cold, began their ride, noting carefully the characteristics of the land as they journeyed eastward. Francis pulled out the military map that

Joe had given him. After he studied it for a few moments, he gathered the men together and said, "The North Canadian River flows to the east, north of us. We crossed it just before getting' to the Cheyenne Agency." Pointing with his right gloved hand, he continued, "That way is the South Canadian. Ahead of us is Cross Timbers. Let's camp when we get to some wooded country. We'll be on the western edge of the Timbers then."

The other members of the delegation, looking like hunched buffaloes perched atop horses, nodded their heads indicating that they understood and agreed. Bernard, pulling one of the pack mules, spurred his horse and cantered until he was alongside Francis. Riding beside him, he nonchalantly said, "Francis, sounds like you've been here before."

"Not me, but Joe," replied Francis. "He and Kate built a cabin last year some place southeast of us." Sleet, blown by a northeast wind, struck his face sharply as he turned and spoke to Bernard. The cold wind and pelting abbreviated any more conversation between the two men. Like the others in the party, they were looking forward to being able to get in a shelter, which they would have to hastily make, so they could escape the wintery elements.

Bright sunshine greeted the men the next morning when they crawled out from under their ice-encrusted bedding. As they were eating breakfast of salt pork and drinking hot coffee, Chief Wiwise spoke, "It's a good day. Grandfather sun is making the ice shine. Three of us will go south for two miles then ride northeast. I'll be one of the south riders. Three men go north. Francis, you lead the riders who go north. Those of you who go north will come to a river. Turn right and follow it to where it meets the road. According to this here map, the road we're on will meet and cross the river. Look at your maps. See what I mean? We'll camp tonight where the road crosses the river and talk about what we saw." Because of Wiwise's status as an elder, no one disagreed with him.

The next day, the men followed a similar plan. Before breaking camp, Chief Wiwise announced that he would lead the pack mules to the next agreed to camping site. "I'll see you where this here road meets a road going north and south. It should be the Arbuckle Wagon Road. It's 'bout six miles ahead" he said and headed east.

A wisp of smoke told those who had ridden to explore the land that paralleled the Cheyenne Agency Wagon Road that they were approaching the pre-determined camp site. It was hard to see because sunlight was fast fading, but the roving riders were delighted when they saw the silhouette of a deer roasting over a fire. Their revered elder was hunkered near the fire poking at it and adding more wood to keep it flaming.

"How did you get it?" questioned Narcis Juneau as he dismounted and tied his horse's reins to an overhanging branch. "I didn't hear a gunshot." Chief Wiwise didn't say anything as he carefully added another log to the camp fire. He merely nodded his head toward his bow and quiver leaning against a nearby oak tree.

While eating, the two groups of explorers excitedly shared their day's adventures and what they had seen along Little River and its numerous tributaries. The fresh venison, combined with spoonfuls of lard and hot coffee soon put most of the men, who had crawled under their blankets, into deep slumber. Snoring came from the men who had positioned themselves near the fire, attempting to keep warm. Only Wiwise and Francis remained awake. Together they worked out plans to explore more of the area. Finally, they too found ways to sleep as the night time temperature fell to near freezing.

****

"Francis, isn't Joe's cabin supposed to be close to Pond Creek? According to the map, this here stream should be Pond Creek. We left the South Canadian River earlier this afternoon," said Clardy. He folded up his now, well-tattered map and shoved it back into a side pocket of his topcoat. After pulling back on his gloves and shifting in his saddle to show his apprehension, he glanced over at Francis and the other delegate who were sitting on their horses alongside him.

****

Five weeks earlier, Chief Wiwise and Francis had agreed, after filling up on roasted deer, the delegates should split up if the region was going to be fully explored. Their decision was made at the camp site where the road they followed through Cross Timbers met the Arbuckle Wagon Road. The next morning, by plan, Wiwise and two other delegates rode north to explore the land between Little River and the North Canadian. Three other delegates, Francis, Bernard Bertrand and Joshua Clardy, headed south. Their responsibility was to examine the area as far south as the main Canadian River. Everyone was instructed to meet back at the first camp site on the Cheyenne Agency Wagon Road in five weeks to share each group's findings and opinions.

****

Francis nudged his horse down the south steep bank of Pond Creek and into the creek's frigid waters. His horse slipped and lunged up the opposite bank. Finally, it managed to clamor up the opposite bank and get its footing on level ground. Reining his horse around, Francis hollered, "Come on! Especially you, Joshua! Don't let the mule balk! When he starts down the bank, drop its lead rope. He'll follow your horse!"

When the other two men were safely across the creek and on their horses beside him, Francis said, "Joe's and Kate's cabin should be north of us. See the hills over there? Joe told me that him and Kate built their cabin at the bottom of some hills about a quarter mile north of Pond Creek."

The men, including Francis, carefully scanned the horizon looking for the cabin, which they hoped to use for the night's shelter. As the sun sank lower in the western horizon and the late afternoon temperature began to drop, Bernard, looking through his binoculars, pointed and shouted, "THERE IT IS!" Spotting what Bernard had seen, Francis and Joshua raced their horses toward the cabin knowing that once inside they could get out of the cold and start a fire. "WAIT!" cried Bernard who was fumbling to put his binoculars back in their case. This was becoming increasingly difficult because his horse began stepping sideways and throwing its head in an effort to dislodge the bit that was holding it back from joining the other horses that were galloping ahead. To make matters worse, no one had grabbed the mule's lead rope. Fortunately, the pack mule started running in the same direction as the equine herd racing to the cabin.

****

"POW! POW!" Bernard and Joshua who were still asleep in the cabin the next morning threw back their blankets, jumped up, grabbed their revolvers and peered out the cabin's windows. More gunshots were heard. Still they saw nothing, but became increasingly edgy. A few minutes later, they relaxed when the cabin door opened and saw Francis. He was shedding his coat and stomping his boots to get off the slight snow that had fallen during the night. "If you can get the fire stoked and the coffee boiling, we gonna have roast rabbit for breakfast," he said grinning. Before him stood two men, holding revolvers and wearing only long johns.

After breakfast, Francis and the two others in his group took time to view the cabin and its surroundings. Francis was struck by the contrast that he saw on the hills, oaks bearing brown leafs, dots of green cedars and barren spots of red sandstone. The valley extending to Pond Creek was grass, no longer verdant but brown and reddish-brown slightly sprinkled with the night's light snowfall.

Joshua and Bernard were swallowing the last of their coffee when Francis hollered, "Let's go! We still need to look at the land west of us before we can swing north and meet up with the rest of the delegation!"

"Where did you say we're to find them?" asked Joshua who was just mounting his horse with the mule's lead rope griped in his left hand.

"At the place where we first camped along the western edge of the Timbers," replied Francis, anxious for Bernard to join him and Joshua. Finally, everyone rode out to explore the southwest region of the land that they were considering for a new reservation.

****

Once the delegation was back at the Cheyenne Agency, it did not take long for the delegates, riding in separate coaches, to get to Abilene even after a stop in the Cherokee Strip. Any notion of taking Cherokee land was discounted after looking at the Cherokee Strip. The men wanted to meet with Mr. Palmer in St. Mary's as a unified party to deliver a consensus suggestion as soon as possible. To accomplish this, the delegates decided before they left the Cherokee Strip that the best way to travel from Abilene would be together on the Atchison, Topeka and Santa Fe Railway. The train briefly stopped in Wamego and, even though Francis was anxious to see Etta, he rode the train through to St. Mary's for the meeting with Mr. Palmer. Upon arrival, the delegates immediately went to Agency Office and handed the Indian Agent a hand-written note detailing the land they wanted for a new reservation:

"On the East by the West line of the Seminoles. On the South by the Cannadian *(Sich!)* river *(Sich!)*, and on the North by the north fork of the Cannadian *(Sich!)* River, and to extend far enough West to Contain 900 sq miles of the aggregate."

Mr. Palmer told the delegates that he would forward their request to Mr. Ely Parker, Indian Commissioner, with a favorable recommendation. The delegates were about to leave when Mr. Palmer advised in a cautionary tone, "Don't expect a quick answer because the Commissioner's in Washington City. It probably will be several months before I hear back from him, but I'll let you know his answer as soon as I get his answer."

It was late in the afternoon and the sun was starting to set when the exploratory delegation finished its business with the Indian Agent. Francis knew that it would take a couple of hours to get a horse and ride back to Wamego. Rather than risk being caught in a snow storm that was threatening to blow in, Francis turned to the other men and said, "I'll go over to Archange's and stay at her place for the night. Any of you want to do the same? I'm sure she won't mind."

Joshua, who lived in Louisville, took Francis up on his offer. Bernard said, "I'm already home so I don't need any place to stay. Thanks anyway." The remaining three delegates lived a short distance east of St. Mary's and individually declined the night's lodging.

Francis and Joshua were glad that they had stayed with Archange and Moke-je-win because four inches of snow blanketed the Oregon Trail the next morning. Where it had drifted, the snow was two feet deep. As they rode west,

Joshua asked, "Do you think the Commisioner'll approve our suggestion?" "Yep!" replied Francis. "When do you think we'll go?" asked Joshua.

"About spring. Not this year, but in about two years."

"Why so long?"

"Some of us got business to take care of. You know — property to sell — things like that. Etta and me will need to sell our allotments."

35 – Seven Families

Francis was not prepared for the homecoming that awaited him in Wamego. He bounded into his house expecting to see Etta and be greeted by her warm personality and cheerful chatty self. Instead he was met by Kate. "Shh," she said as she smiled but gestured quietness. Benjamin was sound asleep in her lap, and Ltl' Joe was playing with the toy wooden horse that Francis had carved for him shortly before Benjamin was born. Thinking that Kate was asking him to be quiet because of Benjamin, Francis asked, "Where's Etta?"

Kate nodded toward the bedroom. "Mother's not well. She's resting. I know that she's anxious for you to get back, but she's worn out."

Francis tiptoed in the direction of the bedroom. Slowly opening the door and peeking in, he saw Etta. She had her eyes closed, but opened them when she heard the door creak. Tears began trickling down the outside corners of her eyes when she saw Francis. Ever so slowly, she mouthed, "*Bozhow.*"

Francis walked over and sat down on the bed beside Etta. He leaned over and tenderly kissed her. In silence, he stroked her still black hair with one hand while holding her folded hands gently with the other.

****

Etta regained some of her strength when the weather improved. Feeling better, she frequently asked Francis about the recommendation the exploratory delegation gave to Mr. Palmer, the Indian Agent. During a discussion toward the end of the summer, Etta asked Francis, "What's taking the agent so long to make up his mind?" "The final decision isn't his," replied Francis.

"Who makes it?" asked Etta.

Sighing to show his own impatience, Francis answered, "The Indian Commissioner."

"Who's that?"

"Ely Parker. He's way off in Washington City. He can't be reached very fast except by a telegram. Guess he also gets mail, but any letter would take a long time to reach him. Perhaps that's what Mr. Palmer did with our delegation's suggestion."

Etta started dwelling on the name, Ely Parker. *"He can't be the Seneca who lived in Galesburg — the one who worked for William Chobart?"* she mused. Coming in from having sat in the sun, she asked Francis, "What do you know about Ely Parker — the Commissioner?"

"Not much," he answered. "Only that he drafted the surrender papers that General Lee signed. He worked for General Grant then. Still does 'cause Grant's the President now and he appointed Parker to be the Indian Commissioner."

"Did either of them used to live in Galesburg, Illinois?" asked Etta.

"I heard that Grant did," replied Francis, looking out the front window. "He went bankrupt there. Say, remember Parker from Galena? The fella that worked for Chobart — you don't suppose —?"

Shifting in the chair where she had sat down next to Francis, Etta got a serious look on her face and said, "Take me to the telegraph office!"

****

Francis loaded all the things he thought he and Etta would need to start their lives on the new reservation in the

Indian Territory. The last two years had not been easy on Etta because of her deteriorating health. She wanted to help Francis pack and load the covered wagon, but did not have the strength. They were preparing to leave the house they had purchased in Wamego shortly before Francis left to explore the Indian Territory. It was their insurance. Both knew that a move was imminent, but they wanted a house to which they could return to if life on the new reservation was not to their satisfaction.

With the wagon loaded, Francis went and got Etta. He boosted her up and into the driver's seat. Thoughtfully, Francis had made a bed of blankets just behind the seat for Etta should she need to rest on the journey. Seeing that everything was ready, Francis shouted "Ha!" and the team of oxen started north towards Louisville.

Etta and Francis rendezvoused with Bat and Mary and their grandsons, Frank and one-month old William, at Matilda's. Kate and Joseph, along with Ltl' Joe and Benjamin, had agreed to meet them there also. In silence and filled with nervousness, they waited for the Anderson's, Clardy's, Pettifer's and Tupin's. Francis thought, *"Seven families and fourteen wagons."*

Not seeing a wagon with Matilda's things in it, Etta leaned over to Francis and whispered. "Isn't Matilda coming with us?"

Francis turned his head and spoke into Etta's ear, "She's coming later with her children — wants to have a house ready for them."

An ox's bellow alerted Francis that the others were nearing Matilda's place. After everyone was assembled, Amable Tupin discretely approached Etta. He looked up at her and quietly said as if embarrassed that others might hear, "Thanks for buying me and my wife a wagon so we could move and for helping us get supplies. Heard that you grub-staked some of the others too. When they have a chance, I'm sure they'll thank you too."

Etta merely nodded her head while carefully looking to see who had arrived. Not seeing Olivie and Archange, she said to Francis, "Olivie and Archange aren't here either!"

Sensing Etta's concern, Francis explained, "Olivie wants to wait until next spring to move. Archange and Moke-je-win will come then too." His words did little to ease Etta's disappointment.

"Francis," said John Anderson in a hushed voice. "Where's Bat's and Mary's son, Joseph?"

Taking John aside and putting his hand on John's shoulder, Francis quietly said, "He died in late 1869, just before I left with the delegation — got pneumonia and died. Mary took it real hard. Don't know 'bout Bat. He didn't say much. The move will good for both of them. Did you see their other children, Francis and William? They had them after they lost Joseph. They call Francis, Frank. He's just over one now."

"Their other son must be a newborn."

"That's William. He was born a few weeks ago."

Hearing that, John broke into a big grin as Francis patted him on the shoulder and turned back to hear what Joe was saying.

"We'll go down the Chisholm Trail. It's the easiest way to take wagons. The land west of the Flint Hills is flatter than on east side. It'll be easier to pull the wagons," said Joe to the group. "Also, if we were to go south from Topeka, there'd be some big rivers, like the Marias des Cygnes, to ford. This time of the year some of 'em might be flooded. Any questions?"

"Not now! Sounds like a good plan," spoke up George Pettifer. Elizabeth, George's wife, nodded her head in agreement with him.

"Wait!" cried out Joshua Clardy. "How we gonna get past all them cattle supposedly comin' up the trail. Heard there's sometimes thousands of them together."

Joe, who in an earlier planning meeting was chosen to guide the Potawatomi to their new reservation, answered the concern in a manner that showed his leadership and experience, "We'll be makin' the trip at a time when the grass is short, but enough for our animals. The herds comin' north need lots of grass to make the long trip. We shouldn't expect to meet any until 'bout when we get to the Cheyenne Agency."

"Where's that?" asked Joshua.

"Northwest of where we're goin'," joined in Francis. "We should get to the agency in late May if we don't get tangled up with any large herds before we get there. The map I'm passin' around shows the agency. It's a little south of the North Canadian River. Our reservation is between that river and the South Canadian, but to the east."

After giving everyone time to look at the tattered map and upon seeing that they were ready, Joe said, "Let's go. We'll spend the first night in Manhattan."

Slowly the vanguard of the Citizen Potawatomi began moving to the new reservation in the Unorganized Indian Territory, which later would become part of Oklahoma. Francis thought to himself, *"It's April 1872. A new page in our history is turning. Hope that Antoine and Mary Bourbonnais and their group won't have any trouble gettin' down there and findin' us."*

36 – The Tornado

After getting to Abilene three days after leaving Louisville, the small group of seven families and their assemblage of cows, horses, dogs and chickens started down the Chisholm Trail. It was a relatively new route but distinctly marked by the thousands of long horns that had been driven north from Texas during the past five years.

The Flint Hills, on the eastern horizon, provided spectacular sunrises. To the west, a flat, slowly rising, but treeless prairie extended as far as one could see. The trip's monotony was broken each evening by beautiful pink and purple sunsets over the western horizon.

There were distractions, especially the macabre sightings of bleached skeletons. Usually, they obviously were of a long-horn steer or cow that had died while being driven from Texas for shipment by railroad to an eastern market. Other remains, especially when numerous, were of buffalo that had been shot as 'sport' by train passengers from the railroads that were increasingly becoming part of the Kansas landscape. Other piles of buffalo bones were the result of the federal policy aimed at killing herds of buffalo to deprive the Plains Indians of food and thereby subdue them.

Etta was struck by the absence of trees, the same as Kate in 1868. She was relieved when she saw a tree line in the direction where the group was headed, knowing that it signified a watering hole or a river crossing. Often it was a place where camping was struck for the night.

Black clouds began forming over the western horizon when the group was a short distance north of the river crossing at Newton. Francis pulled his wagon up beside Joe's and hollered, "Been watchin' what I see?"

Joe answered back, "Think we should find shelter?"

"Where?"

Etta also was watching the approaching storm. Aware of the possible danger, she suggested sheltering in a valley, a short distance to the east of the Chisholm Trail. "Don't get under or close to any of the trees that are there!" she yelled to Joe.

Not hearing what Etta said, Joe drove his wagon to get under a large cottonwood tree. Kate turned to him and said in a scolding voice, "Do as mother said! Get out from under the tree!"

Twelve minutes later, a driving rain pelted the wagons and exposed livestock. Suddenly, darkness came over the group. A lightning bolt struck a cottonwood tree, stripping off a long section of its bark. Flying pieces of bark smashed against Joe's and Kate's wagon. Just then, Etta, looking up, saw a black, whirling cloud skimming over the tops of the trees when a lightning flash illuminated the sky. People curled up and covered their heads as winds from the tornado shook the wagons. Mothers with young children clutched them to their bosoms in an effort to protect them. In a few moments, the wind ceased, but rain fell throughout the night and the next day.

****

A rooster in a cage tied to one of the wagons fluffed its wet feathers and crowed at daybreak, stirring Etta and Francis from their sleep. The rain had stopped. Finally, two days after the storm swept over the area, bright sunlight and a beautiful blue sky, dotted by fluffy, white clouds greeted the people. Accompanied by singing meadow larks, the adults and older children set about drying out their gear and repairing the coverings on their wagons. Francis and the other men were relieved to find that the heavy rains had not dampened their crop seed.

After examining their seed, Francis and Joe strolled over to the Chisholm Trail. It was extremely muddy and filled with countless water puddles. The trail looked like an impassable wide swath of water-filled cow tacks and shimmering wagon wheel ruts through a sea of green, springtime prairie.

"Think the oxen can pull the wagons through this stuff?" asked Joe. Tipping back his hat and sipping fresh, hot coffee, Francis in a somewhat ambivalent tone responded, "It'll be tough on them. If it gets too bad, we can stop and wait for the trail to dry out."

Etta often chatted with Francis over the next few days, in part to keep his mind off the torture being endured by the oxen as they slogged through the mud. However, as the group drew closer to the boundary of Indian Territory, Francis noticed that her talking became more and more abbreviated and less frequent. Often, she would crawl over the back of the seat and lie down in the bed of blankets and straw that Francis had made. During the times that Etta was resting, Francis entertained himself by humming or singing the French songs he had learned while growing up near Saint Hyacinthe, Quebec. Sometimes the others heard him and joined in.

****

Before breaking camp in southern Kansas near Caldwell, where they had spent two days resting the oxen, Joe said, "Our first night in Indian Territory will be in what's called the Cherokee Strip. We'll find water and a place to stop at a stream called the Salt Fork. It'll be a long day, but we'll make it."

Francis quickly interjected, "The government wanted to put our new reservation in the northern part of Indian

Territory and take land away from the Cherokee, but me and the rest of the men who came down here a couple of years ago didn't like the area. It's too barren. You'll like where our reservation is much better. It has lots of timber, wild animals for food and good water and farm land."

****

"Whoa," commanded Francis to his oxen as he pulled on the ropes attached to their noses. It was late in the afternoon. He saw that Joe was stopping his team in a wooded area beside a stream and knowingly asked Joe, "Isn't this the Salt Fork stop?"

Joe was turned around in his seat, pitching camping gear out of his wagon, but Kate caught her father's attention and nodded her head affirmatively because she knew that Joe didn't hear him.

Francis threw his arm over the back of seat and gently shook Etta who earlier in the afternoon had crawled into her bed and fallen asleep. "We're in the Indian Territory," he whispered

37 – Arbuckle Wagon Road

The rapid gunfire made Francis tense. It immediately brought back the horrors of the Westport battle during the Civil War. Joe, in the lead wagon also became very concerned, especially for the safety of those trailing behind him, and stopped.

The shooting came when the Citizen Potawatomi, moving from Kansas, were approaching the North Canadian River crossing. Plans were for them to stop for rest and procure supplies at the Cheyenne Agency a few miles beyond the crossing. However, Joe didn't want to lead the wagon train into a raging gun battle that seemed to have erupted ahead.

Joe, turning and leaning sideways over his wagon so he could be seen and heard by those behind him, yelled, "ANDERSON AND CHARLES! GET UP HERE! FAST!"

"WHICH ANDERSON?" shouted a voice from a trailing wagon.

"PETE!"

Charles was riding his gelding next to his mother and father's wagon, which was two wagons behind the lead. Quickly, he spurred his horse forward to the wagon carrying Joe and his family. Pete handed his team's reins to his wife and jumped to the ground. Bridling and untying his riding horse that was trailing his wagon, he leaped on it bareback and galloped forward to join Charles who already was talking to Joe.

Joe, looking in the direction that the gunfire was coming from, nervously gave orders to Charles and Pete, "Scout out what's happenin'! Don't get in the fight! Stay alive so you can come back and report to me!" With a nod of his head to the left, he added, "I'm gonna take the wagons to the thicket over yonder and try to get behind it! We'll hide best we can! At least we'll have some protection if needed! Suggest that you head that way too and come up the river bank from the east to where the shooting is coming from!"

Joe started heading the wagon train toward the safety of the thicket when he heard bellowing and saw a massive cattle herd slowly walking north. Flanking the herd were cowboys emitting their distinctive "Yippee Yi Yays" and shaking the loops of their lariats. Seeing the size of the herd, Joe kept coursing to the thicket so that his wagon train would not be surrounded by the enormous cattle herd moving north.

Meanwhile, Charles and Pete made their way to the north bank of the river. After tying their horses out of sight, they stealthily crept forward making sure that their movements were concealed by the willows that grew abundantly along the river bank. Ever so slowly, they crawled along the bank until the river crossing was clearly visible. During their careful approach, the shooting stopped. Instead of stillness and quietness, there seemed to be much commotion caused by shouting and the bellowing of cattle. Also, the ground began to shake.

"I don't think we got a problem!" said Pete as he stood, up clearly making himself visible to anyone near the crossing. "What you doin'?" implored Charles in a hushed voice. He tugged at Pete's belt in an effort to get him to get him down and not be seen. Pete didn't budge and began laughing. "Look!" he said. "It's one of them cattle drives!"

Charles and Pete walked back to their horses, chagrined but somewhat humored by what they had seen. As they approached the wagons, Joe said with a grin on his face, "We'll wait here. It'll take awhile for all the cattle to get across. Don't want to get in the middle of 'em."

"What was all the shootin' for?" asked Charles.

"The drovers do it to chase their cattle across a big

river crossing," answered Joe. Standing up, he hollered to the rest of the group, "WHEN WE CAN CROSS THE RIVER, WE'LL GO TO THE CHEYENNE AGENCY! AFTER WE GET RESTED, WE'LL GET ON THE CHEYENNE AGENCY WAGON ROAD AND TAKE IT TO OUR RESERVATION! WE'RE ONLY 'BOUT FOUR DAYS FROM ME AND KATE'S CABIN!"

****

The wagons entered a clearing mid-afternoon in late May. The group had camped by Little Creek the night before. Just as Joe and Kate turned west in the clearing and off the Arbuckle Wagon Road they heard Francis holler, "HOLD UP!" Stopping his wagon, Joe let Francis pull up beside him. Francis leaned over Etta so Joe could hear him better and said, "Me and Etta are stopping here. There's a little spring over there, other side of the clearing. I saw it when I came down with the delegation. Told myself then that this'd be a nice place to settle if given the chance."

Joe looked around and said, "Guess that means that you're not comin' any farther. I agree. This is a nice place. I'll come by in a few days to see how you're doin'. Take good care of Etta and Charles."

Several members of the group, who were on horseback, rode up to hear Francis and Joe. Joe turned to them and said, "Etta and Francis are stopping here. You and the others are welcome to come with me and Kate or you can find a place to stop. You might want to wait 'til mornin' to look for your own places to settle down. If you decide to come along with me and Kate — we're about three or so miles from the cabin -- there'll be some rough goin' but we need to get past a deep ravine. You'll soon see our cabin when we turn south and go down a hill."

Etta and Francis waved good-bye as the small group of the remaining wagons disappeared down a slight hill and into the woods that flanked the west side of the clearing.

38 – Lifeless Body

"IT'S DONE!" Francis excitedly hollered. Etta, who was tending the garden that she and Francis had planted soon after they settled, looked up. She saw Francis and Charles standing on the roof of their dog-trot log cabin they built slightly west of the Arbuckle Wagon Road. Because of her health, Etta had to rely on her husband and son to do the heavy work, even most of the garden work, especially as the summer heat became intensive and gruesome later in the summer.

"It still don't have no windows," she said as she wiped her hands on her day dress and started walking to the cabin.

"I know," replied Francis, climbing down his makeshift ladder. "We'll still have to use the oil cloth 'til I can get some glass. At least the cloth lets in some light and will keep out any cold winds that'll be blowin' in a few months." Just then he remembered something Joe told him two days ago. "Joe's going to the Cheyenne Agency next week. Maybe I can go with him and can get some glass along with any other supplies that we need."

"Want me and Charles to stay here by ourselves?"

Aware of Etta's concern, Francis said, "I think Bat's goin' too. Between the three of us and the supplies, the wagon will be full, especially when we come back. Want to go stay with Kate? She and Mary would be glad to have you visit 'til we get back. I'll take you over there in a couple of days. Charles can take care of the livestock and the chickens."

****

The springtime sun reflected off the glass windows in the cabin as Joe and Charles rode up the wooded hill west of where Etta and Francis settled. "Thanks again for your helpin' me clear out some of my woods," Joe said. "I know that Bat appreciated the help you gave to him and Mary too. I know that they'll be glad when they can move out of their dugout." "Couldn't work the fields — too wet from the spring rains to do any plowing. Wanted to do somethin'. Glad to have helped," replied Charles.

"Strange," said Joe in a kidding tone, "that you knew to come the same time as the Lasley girl."

Charles blushed.

Just as they were about to leave the tree line, three sharp shots rang out. POW! POW! POW! The reports made their horses flinch and throw back their heads. Both Joe and Charles almost instinctively tightened their grips on the reins and pulled them back slightly to keep control of their horses.

Charles remarked, "Uncle Joe, father's probably out shootin' something to eat. Maybe he got some rabbits." Both men laughed lightly. "Yeah!" said Joe. "It'll be nice to get something fresh besides chicken. How'd he know we're comin' and would be hungry."

Ducking their heads under the overhanging oak branches at the edge of the clearing, Joe and Charles looked up and saw a horrific sight. Francis was struggling to get himself free of a lariat and out of a mud pit. Etta was standing over a man not far from Francis. She held a knife in one hand and a bloody scalp in the other. Another man, was galloping south down the Arbuckle Wagon Road, bent over and bleeding from his left shoulder.

Seeing the scene, Joe and Charles raced to Etta and Francis. Quickly, they jumped off their horses. Joe helped Francis get up and loose from the rope that bound him while Charles ran to Etta who was standing over the dead man on the ground. At the moment, Etta was in her own mind, recalling why her tribal name, Watchekee, was deemed important "A woman named Watchekee once saved her tribe," she muttered while recalling what her grandmother told her.

Cautiously, Charles took the knife that his mother was brandishing. Etta handed him the scalp, which he laid on the dead man's torso. Etta kept looking back at the lifeless figure on the ground, but was unusually calm as Charles led her to the cabin. Meanwhile, Francis, muddied and bearing rope burns, came over to the scene of the downed man. Joe started helping Francis, who was breathing hard, and excitedly asked, "What happened?" Francis did not reply, but instead pushed Joe away and hurried to the cabin to check on Etta.

She was holding her chest and sweating. Etta was trying to conceal the pain that had erupted in her chest from the excitement of the ruckus that had unfolded just moments earlier. Breathlessly, she started to explain what happened to her son and Joe, "Francis went out to check the field to see it was dry enough to be plowed. I was inside working when I heard laughing and voices. I looked outside and saw Francis – – roped and bein' drug through the mud. I grabbed the rifle by the door — and hurried outside. Shot the one who was draggin' Francis.— He fell off his horse! The other man shot at me! I shot back — didn't knock him off his horse, but he slumped and runoff. I must've gone back inside and got my knife and sc…."

"Never mind, mother!" said horror-stricken Charles.

Etta was wiping the mud off Francis when he said, "Was scared I was gonna get shot!" Looking at her, he breathlessly remarked, "Thought I was when you fired. Your shootin' saved me."

Joe and Charles went outside to discuss what they should do. Francis was too exhausted from his ordeal and stayed inside with Etta. Joe said to Charles, "Somehow we gotta' get rid of the guy before some US Marshall comes along. Think he might understand why Etta shot 'em, but the scalpin' might be a problem! Get the horses harnessed and hitched to a wagon. We'll load him up and dump him in the woods a ways east of us. The red wolves and buzzards will take care of him after a short time."

Before the man's body was hoisted up and into the wagon, Joe rolled it over to see if he recognized the man. Joe stiffened and stood up. — "I've seen him before! He's the drifter who fell off his horse after Kate shot! Look at the ugly scar on his forehead — above the left eye! The scar's U-shaped! His horse must've kicked him! Me and Kate thought she'd grazed him! " he said.

Working together, Joe and Charles heaved the dead man into the wagon bed. "Mustn't forget his scalp!" said Charles as he winced, picked up the scalp and threw it onto the bloody body in the wagon.

Returning to the cabin one hour later, Charles and Joe opened the door. Charles started to say, "We dumped him in the woods east of ...." He and his uncle suddenly halted. On the kitchen floor was Francis, cradling Etta's body. With tear-stained eyes, he distraughtly looked up and softly said, "She collapsed just after you left."

****

Joe quickly rode home to tell Kate and Bat of their mother's death. Bat and Mary had just returned from visiting the Clardy's. Once everyone was assembled, they made a solemn but hurried trip to console Francis. Upon arriving, Francis and Charles quietly were sitting at the kitchen table. Etta's body, which lay on her bed, was covered with a blanket. Nothing was said about the drifters that Etta had confronted. The only thing Francis, who by now was wearing clean clothes, said when rest of his family came in was, "I found this leather pouch under her pillow. It was empty except for this here note."

"Note? What's it say?" asked Bat.

"It's a receipt from Hank's Livery back in Louisville."

Not understanding, Kate wrinkled her brow as she looked at the blanket draped body of her mother and quizzically asked in between broken sobs, "Receipt for what?"

"Six wagons and ox teams," softly said Francis as he turned his head and stared into the lifeless face of his beloved Etta.

Made in the USA
Charleston, SC
21 April 2013